CW00323099

A FIREFIGHTER
CHRISTMAS
CAROL
AND
OTHER STORIES

Copyright ©2021 by Douglas R. Brown

All rights reserved.
ISBN: 978-1-7368820-0-9

DEDICATION

I dedicate this collection to all the first responders who keep us safe every day. Your job is a hard one, both mentally and physically. Through all the trials and tribulations, you are always there for your fellow man, and for that I thank you.

I'd also like to give a special shout out to my cousin, Greg Ecleberry. I have always looked up to Greg from the days when we collected the same Star Wars toys to now when he is a Battalion Chief at a great fire department. Greg has watched me go through my ordeal with a unique perspective, and we are forever linked by what we have witnessed throughout our careers. Thank you, Greg, for always being there.

Epertase Publishing
First American Edition

This is a work of fiction. Names, characters, places, and incidents either are the product of the author's imagination or are used fictitiously. Any resemblance to actual events, locales, or persons, living or dead, is entirely coincidental. *A Firefighter Christmas Carol* is a reimagining of Charles Dickens' *A Christmas Carol*.

Copyright ©2021 by Douglas R. Brown
Editing by Rebecca Brown

Cover art and author photo by Steve Murphy.

All rights reserved.
No part of this book may be reproduced, scanned, or distributed in any printed or electronic form without permission. Please do not participate in or encourage piracy of copyrighted materials in violation of the author's rights. Purchase only authorized editions.
Visit Douglas R. Brown at epertasepublishing.com
Follow Douglas on Twitter @douglasrbrown22
Like Epertase on Facebook
Contact Douglas at epertase@gmail.com
ISBN 13: 978 1 7368820 0 9

A NOTE FROM THE AUTHOR

Thank you for taking the time to check out my collection of short stories.

First is the feature story, a reimagining of Charles Dickens's classic novella *A Christmas Carol.* In *A Firefighter Christmas Carol,* Elliot's PTSD replaces Scrooge's greed as our protagonist's personal demon.

Next up is *Janitor.* Jeb enjoys working nights as a janitor in an empty factory until he realizes he's not alone.

In *Death Alarm*, what happens when pure evil targets members of one of the noblest professions?

CatchTime explores how a single nasty comment on a social media platform is all it takes to really get under a guy's skin.

Skelwaller Lane shows how even the most brutal behavior can sometimes seem justified if the entire story is told.

Closing out the collection is *DOA,* a spooky little tale about a paramedic with a haunting secret.

Join me as I delve into the psychological with an occasional assist from the supernatural.

ACKNOWLEDGEMENTS

Before we go any further, I would like to thank a few people. First, thank you to my proofreaders, Battalion Chief Greg Ecleberry, my mother Lillian Dove, Firefighter David Signet, Deputy Chief Sean Wooten, Bobbe Ecleberry, Lieutenant Phil Biggs, Cindy Busi, and Retired Firefighter Kelly McClellan. I would also like to thank City of Columbus Employee Assistance Program Director Lisa Callander and Columbus, Ohio Division of Fire Chief Jeffrey Happ for their invaluable help on this project.

I am especially appreciative of everyone who has supported my writing career. An author's career is sometimes a lonely one. Your support is what allows me to have the strength to put my writing out there.

Thank you to my wife, Angie, and son, Aiden, for being my world.

There are a few people who have been instrumental to what you see in my finished work, and nothing would be as polished or professional without them.

If you have fallen as much in love with my covers as I have, then you know Steve Murphy is to thank. Steve has become a dear friend in the course of creating my gorgeous covers and he leaves me breathless each and every time. I can't thank him enough.

I have heard it said that an author is nothing without a good editor. I have also heard that the editor is always right. Both of those statements are true and the sooner a budding author realizes it, the better his or her writing will be.

Early in my career, my aunt Bobbe Ecleberry tried

to teach me these lessons. Being deathly protective of my "children," I didn't always listen. She probably banged her head against the wall many times trying to get something through my head. I know how to write because of you, Bobbe. I will forever be thankful and continue to eagerly await your reactions to what I have written.

And finally, Rebecca Brown. We first worked together on *Tamed* and *The Rise of Cridon.* Years later, I reconnected with Rebecca at the beginning of the pandemic and asked her to give a fresh look to all my work, both existing and future. Becca, you have been nothing short of a genius. When we butt heads on my use of "concepts that are just cool" versus "what is actually necessary or appropriate," my work is always better when I heed your advice. We may not always agree, but your red pen beatdowns have made me too weary to argue, like a boxer in the later rounds. Of course, I'm kidding. I can't thank you enough for what you've done.

What I'm saying is, when you read my work, it is a combination of several people with talent. I thank you all. And wait until you see what's coming.

A FIREFIGHTER
CHRISTMAS
CAROL

*Content warning: If you're depressed, or you have lost someone to suicide, or you're a first responder, or from the military, and reading about horrible experiences that are sometimes graphic might hit too close to home for you, please don't continue any further. While I wrote *A Firefighter Christmas Carol* in hopes of helping people better understand PTSD and what to look for in your friends, family, and coworkers, I fully realize it may be too raw for some. It was almost too raw for me to write. This story may not be for you. If, however, you press on, I hope I did this topic justice. If you think my novella might help someone else, please share.

FOREWORD

Charles Dickens wrote his novella *A Christmas Carol* in 1843 over the course of six weeks. Since that time, the story of a greedy old man named Ebenezer Scrooge has been adapted and reimagined countless times across all types of media. The following story is my own reimagining with a modern flare and a slightly different message. I believe it is one that Charles Dickens himself would understand.

In 1865, Charles Dickens was involved in a fatal train crash in which seven carriages plunged over a bridge that was being repaired. Dickens was in the only first-class carriage not to plunge over the edge. As he was one of the few to escape serious injury, he began tending to the wounded. In a sense, Mr. Dickens became a first responder at his own accident. One gentleman had a laceration on his head so severe that Dickens had to look away. Using a hat to hold water, he washed off some of the blood and calmed the man with a sip of brandy from a flask. The man died during Dickens's care. A woman he tried to help also died shortly after. Ten people died that day, and forty more were injured. After such a traumatic near-death experience, Charles Dickens suffered lingering aftereffects that, in modern times, we label as Post-Traumatic Stress Disorder or PTSD.

It's normal after going through something traumatic to experience some symptoms of Post-Traumatic Stress (PTS) that eventually go away on their own. It's when those symptoms don't resolve or get worse and start to meaningfully interfere with your life, work, and relationships that it becomes concerning. Symptoms of PTS could be anything from an increased heartrate in stressful situations to increased anxiety when placed in a similar situation to the one that caused the symptoms in the first place. Feeling anxious or leery of going into a swimming pool after almost drowning could be an example of PTS. Waking up in the middle of the night unable to breathe after having nightmares of drowning would more likely fall under PTSD. Judging from Dickens's own words a few years after the accident, his PTS symptoms had progressed into PTSD.

In 1868, Dickens wrote, "I have sudden vague rushes of terror, even when riding in a hansom cab, which are perfectly unreasonable but quite insurmountable." His son told of Dickens gripping carriage seats in a state of utter panic at the slightest jolts and at least once throwing himself onto the isle floor in fear the train was about to crash.

Most people experience some form of PTS in their lives. Some of those people go on to suffer from PTSD: First responders, parents who lose children, soldiers, witnesses of horrible tragedies, as well as many others. In the fire service, we struggle with PTSD on a catastrophic level. Firefighters across the world commit suicide at an alarming rate each year. I have lost half a dozen friends on the Columbus Fire Department alone. In Columbus, Ohio we are fortunate to have an administration that strives to understand this issue and has devoted resources to helping fight it. We have a wonderful Critical Incident Stress Debriefing Team, an Employee Assistance Program, and support from all levels of our leadership. Despite this, we still lose members to suicide, sometimes more than one a year, and it is devastating.

There are many reasons this is a difficult problem to address. I won't list them all here, but I'd like to mention a couple. A lot of times, the person suffering from PTSD isn't even aware that they are in as dire straits as they are. Or they may believe they are still experiencing the more common symptoms of PTS and things will get better on their own like they have in the past. Most firefighters think of themselves as strong and not susceptible to such "weaknesses" without understanding that there is nothing weak about it. After all, firefighters are inherently fixers and not used to "needing fixed."

The effects of PTSD and the progression from PTS may come on fast or slowly over time like the proverbial frog in a pot of water. By the time the person suffering realizes there is a problem, the water might already be boiling.

That's part of what might have happened to me.

After an accident that killed a little boy close to my son's age, I unknowingly started down that path. While I had seen other children die in my career (too many), there was something different in how that particular call played out. I won't get into details here, but a keen eye will be able to put some of the pieces together as they read through this story.

Here's the pisser about trying to self-recognize PTSD: It isn't always one event that brings it on. For me, I had nearly twenty years with the fire service, seeing everything you can imagine. My feelings of sadness usually faded over time, but they could have been lingering in the back of my mind for years. That call could have been the sole catalyst for what happened to me or simply the terrible, life-altering tipping point after years of buildup. I can't know for sure. Whatever the reason, my symptoms weren't getting better over time.

In the weeks, months, and years that followed, several things happened. First, I started writing as a cathartic way of escaping my feelings. Second, I neglected my family to the point of nearly losing my marriage and basically missing a year or so of my son's life. I remember responding to one particular report of an auto accident involving children that filled me with unbelievable dread while sitting in the passenger seat of the medic truck. I had to concentrate on calming my breaths and fighting the urge to simply stay in the truck once we arrived on scene. Though that call didn't turn out to be serious and I quickly reverted to doing my job, it was almost overwhelming for a few seconds. I wondered how I could keep working.

You have to understand I didn't know I was broken. I mean, sure, I knew my world was falling apart around me, but my brain constantly told me I was fine. Or I would be fine. I was the strong one, after all. I never let the shit get to me before and it wasn't getting to me then. It couldn't. Friends even told me I was acting differently, but what did they know, right? They didn't know what was in my head.

Or did they?

I'm one of the lucky ones. I was able to recognize what was happening to me at some point and I had resources to help. Not everyone is so fortunate.

I'm better now. I came out the other end better equipped to recognize my triggers, and now I use what I learned to help others when I see in them what in hindsight I saw in my younger self.

I started my take on Charles Dickens's wonderful Christmas tale with the idea of helping people better understand PTSD while giving a unique take on his story. What it turned into was, in a strange and unexpected way, a piece of me. Not exactly how things happened for me, of course, but enough.

The first full book I ever wrote was called *Slow Burn*. In a clumsy, amateurish way, *Slow Burn* attempted to show how the terrible things I saw as a first responder almost broke me as a person. It was a good idea, but poorly done. I'm thankful that it only lives on my computer and in my heart and not out in the world. Thanks to Charles Dickens's inspiration, I believe that with this story I have succeeded in writing what I wanted to write all those years back.

While I never reached the point of contemplating suicide, it wasn't because I'm stronger than anyone else or any garbage like that. It was because of luck, my own personal circumstances, and getting the help I needed when I needed it.

If you are struggling with PTSD, depression, or suicidal thoughts, you need to know that people care about you. You may not believe that right now, but you are special in this world, and this world is better because you're in it. The ways I got better were unique to me and my circumstances, and the ways you can get better might be completely different, but the trick is recognizing that you *can* get better and finding the ways that work for you.

Sometimes the path to suicide feels inevitable. Even if you read nothing else I ever write, read this: It is not inevitable. I'll say it again. Suicide is not inevitable. That path needs broken somehow so you can see it from a different angle. A lot of times, it can't be done on your own. I don't care how "strong" you are.

If you've prepared a plan to kill yourself or even

consider it on occasion, please call 1-800-273-8255 right now or visit suicidepreventionlifeline.org before it's too late. Your life matters more than you know. There are good things for you still. You just can't see them right now because they're hiding behind a mountain. But they are there. You're not weak. You just need what we all need sometimes: help.

Good luck. I'm pulling for you.

STAVE ONE
THE GUIDE

The wobbly, broken tone of the medic alarm blared from the firehouse loudspeaker overhead. The computerized voice of the dispatcher reported another ill person, this one on Beaker Street. It was 3:16 AM on a cold and snowy night. Elliot had only just closed his eyes an hour before after transporting a patient to the hospital. He felt like he hadn't slept a wink.

He sat up and rubbed his tired eyes with his palms. They didn't want to open. He would have given anything for just a couple hours of shut-eye. Twenty-four-hour shifts were a bear without at least a nap. His body was exhausted. His tangled brain was exhausted. He tried to focus on getting up. It wasn't just missing sleep on one night that was killing him. Sleep on his days off had been elusive for months. He'd spent many nights staring at the digital red block numbers of his alarm clock. If he didn't get some sleep soon, nature would ensure he did one way or another.

He silently cursed the EMS gods as he swung his legs off the bed and shoved his feet into his slip-on boots. With his elbows on his knees, he rubbed his buzzed, receding hair.

He could hear his medic partner, Carl, rustling a few bunks over. He wished Carl were his friend

1

Jimmy instead. Carl stumbled past his bunk to the double doors that led to the apparatus bay while pulling his sweatshirt over his head.

Elliot grabbed his own sweatshirt from the chair beside his bed and stood up, his eyes still refusing to open all the way. As he slogged past his locker, he grabbed his fire department embroidered beanie from inside and then slammed the metal door shut with a bang that echoed through the bunk room. He didn't care if it gave the engine or ladder crew a jolt. If he had to be up, they might as well be up, too.

Just outside the double doors was an artificial Christmas tree that stood to his waist. Colorful decorative lights twinkled across the silver tinsel. He considered kicking the tree over just to spite the season, but the rest of the crew would know it was him and he wasn't up for the complaining that would follow.

The holidays hadn't been the same since Jimmy had swallowed a buckshot on Christmas Eve seven years before. Sometimes when emergency calls woke Elliot in the middle of the night, for the briefest of seconds he still expected to see his old medic partner waiting at the truck. The disappointment of seeing Carl each time never truly faded. Good ol' boring Carl.

Elliot walked like a zombie past the back of the ladder truck to the medic truck where Carl was already waiting in the driver's seat. He pulled his beanie over his head when a chill ran down his neck from the opening bay door. The cold was enough to freeze a dog's piss before the splatter hit the sidewalk. He hated his job.

The snow fell in quarter-sized flakes, covering the grass but not yet sticking to the wet roads. The truck's heater vents blew air as chilly as the outside. Elliot closed the one blowing on his face, at least until the engine warmed up. Neither he nor Carl spoke while en route. Elliot sat with one foot on the dash, which was a terrible idea in the event that a crash inflated the airbags and fed him his knee. It had become yet another bad habit in a string of them.

Carl slowed and asked, "Do you see an address?"

Elliot blinked the sleep from his crusty eyes and tried to focus. He caught a house number. "Three-fifty-seven," he said. "What're we lookin' for?"

Carl squinted as he scanned the numbers. "Three-seventy-five . . . There. The blue house." He stopped in front of the driveway of a quaint one-story home with a string of Christmas lights hanging along the gutter and an illuminated Frosty the Snowman blowup decoration on the front lawn. A bucket of salt with a small shovel sat on the porch. It was one of the nicer houses on a block full of shitholes. In Elliot's time at Station 22, neighborhoods with nice houses interspersed with rundowns had become a familiar sight. Carl once told him it was an unfortunate result of falling house prices in a neighborhood of elderly people. "As the original homeowners died off," he'd said, "their houses were sold cheap or rented out to the lowest bidders. And renters in those neighborhoods don't take much pride in the upkeep." Carl spouted a lot of facts whether Elliot wanted to hear them or not.

Carl grabbed the first aid kit from the side compartment while Elliot reached for his report computer on the wall-mounted charger. It didn't release right away, so he yanked and cursed until it wiggled free.

Freshly laid salt littered the walkway. The front

door was unlocked. Carl opened it slightly and called out, "Fire Department." Then he pushed it open.

Elliot was tired, cranky, and as cold as a polar bear's ass. He sniffled and wiped his nose on a wadded-up tissue from his pocket. To make the night worse, he was probably coming down with a cold. The tickle in his throat he'd noticed before going to bed had extended to a garbage taste in his mouth. He'd probably gotten it from one of his earlier patients. Yet another gift he took from the job.

"You have any gum?" he asked as they walked through the doorway. His voice was tired and scratchy.

"Nope," Carl answered.

"Oh well." Elliot figured his gnarly breath was his patient's problem now.

A little old lady sat in the dark, swallowed in a blue recliner in the front room. The TV was on, a black-and-white movie sending flickering light across the lady's robe. The sound was muted.

"Come in, honey," she said, her voice frail and jittery. "You didn't slip on the front porch, did you?"

Before Carl could answer, Elliot crowded past. "What do you want?" he snapped. He stood with his arms crossed as she looked up at him. Carl flipped on a floor lamp next to her chair.

Her hand touched her chest. "Oh. I . . . uh . . . I'm sorry to bother you." She scratched her arm nervously. A home blood pressure cuff rested on a dinner tray beside the recliner. Next to the cuff was a notepad with notations written in red pen. The shaky lettering looked like someone had been driving down a bumpy road when they wrote it. One column had dates, the next column had times, and the final column had blood pressure readings. Some of the dates were cluttered with as many as twelve or thirteen readings.

Elliot skimmed to the most recent. It read: Dec. 21st – 2:58 AM – 178/92. "Well?" he prompted.

Carl knelt next to the chair. "What's your name, ma'am?" he asked warmly.

"Gladys," she answered.

He removed a blood pressure cuff and stethoscope from the emergency kit. "I'm going to check your vital signs, if that's okay, Gladys."

Gladys nodded.

Elliot sniffled. Uninterested, he asked, "So, what's the major emergency tonight?"

Gladys glanced at him, then looked at Carl, and then back to Elliot again. She wore dark-rimmed glasses and a pink full-length robe. Her voice quivered when she answered, "I … I'm sorry I bothered you two young men. I …"

Carl started to answer, but Elliot interrupted. "Well, it's too late to be sorry now. We're here. So, what do you want?" He yawned and didn't try to hide it.

With his stethoscope pressed against the inside of Gladys's elbow, Carl listened for the faint tick of the blood pressure's top number. Elliot rolled his eyes. What a pointless exercise.

Gladys continued, "I've been checking my blood pressure all night and it's getting higher."

Elliot let his report computer drop to his waist. "Of course it is. Didn't you know that taking your blood pressure over and over in the same arm can give you false readings?"

Gladys shook her head.

"Well, it can. Why'd you wait until three in the morning to call us?"

"I don't know … I—"

"Does your chest hurt or anything like that?"

Gladys rubbed her sternum with her fingers. "I don't think so."

"You just called because your pressure's up, then?"

"It scared me."

"At three in the morning?"

"My doctor said to keep an eye on it."

"Did you call *him*?"

She shook her head.

"What's her pressure, Carl?"

"One-sixty-two over eighty-eight."

Elliot lifted his computer and pecked at the screen with the stylus. "See? It's fine, Gladys. A little high, but fine."

Gladys rubbed her neck with a shaky hand. She smiled at Carl. "You were here before, weren't you?"

Carl smiled back. "Maybe. I'm afraid I don't remember, though. I meet a lot of people."

"You helped my husband when he fell."

Carl nodded. "Oh yeah, I kind of remember." He was probably lying.

Gladys bowed her head a little. "My Harold. He died at the hospital the next day. I miss him so much."

Carl gently touched her hand. "I'm so sorry."

Elliot shuffled side to side, ready to get back to the station. Gladys seemed to dismiss him to focus on Carl. "The doctor said he had bleeding in his brain from the fall. The blood thinners probably caused it. This will be my first Christmas without him in almost sixty years."

Elliot interrupted. "Is anything else bothering you tonight?"

Gladys rubbed her forehead again and looked up.

"I've been a little dizzy lately."

"Anxiety," Elliot snapped. "You've gotten yourself all worked up. You'll be fine. Just go to sleep."

Carl leaned closer to Gladys and asked, "Are you a diabetic, ma'am?"

She nodded.

"Do you mind if I check your sugar?"

She held out her left pointer finger—she knew the routine.

While Carl prepared the tester, Elliot continued pecking at the report computer. "Name?"

"Gladys."

"I know that. What's your last name?"

"Oh. I'm sorry. Berger. Gladys Berger."

He tapped the stylus on the screen. "Date of birth?"

Gladys answered each question. Once Elliot had the information he needed, including a shaky signature from her confirming she didn't want to go to the hospital, he turned toward the door. Without looking back, he said, "A lot of people have real emergencies, Gladys. Checking vital signs at three in the morning doesn't seem like an emergency to most people." The storm door slammed shut behind him.

He finished the report in the truck while Carl did who knew what inside. Elliot was two seconds away from blaring the air horn to light a fire under his partner's ass when Carl stepped out of the house. He spread some salt on the porch before taking his time getting to the truck. He was seething when he climbed into the driver's seat. Elliot couldn't care less. Carl's hand hesitated on the gear shifter and he took a deep breath. "You nearly made her cry," he said without looking over.

"You're not tired of all the bullshit runs, Carl?"

"She's a little old lady, man. She's lonely and

scared. Her husband just died, for Christ's sake. You could try and be a little less of a dick."

"Whatever. You know she didn't need us."

"Maybe not medically, but we still could have done some good for her."

Elliot rolled his eyes and continued pecking away at the computer screen while Carl drove back to the station. Neither of them said another word.

Instead of going back to bed, Elliot sat in a recliner in the TV room and dozed until the 7:00 AM announcement woke him again. He kicked the footrest down and stumbled into the kitchen for some coffee. One of the newer guys was sitting at the table, mug in hand. "Good morning," the new guy said. He had James Dean hair and a smile that lit women on fire. He even had dimples.

Fucking dimples.

Elliot didn't have patience for the new guys. All they wanted to do was train and rah, rah, rah the fire department. He ignored him and went straight for the mugs. After pouring his coffee, adding a splash of whole milk, and stirring in some Sweet 'N Low, he glanced at the news on the TV. The anchors wore ugly Christmas sweaters and talked about the latest Elf on the Shelf craze. He couldn't believe either of those stupid trends had caught on. Nothing but holiday cheer cluttering the airwaves. Wasn't there a train wreck somewhere they could talk about? The next story was breaking news about a fatal police shooting. Some crazy guy fell over his balcony after being shot in his own apartment or something like that.

Now that's more like it. From elves on shelves to police shooting people, all in one segment. *What a world.* At least the anchor was wearing her fun sweater.

"Hey, Elliot," the new guy called before Elliot could get out of the room.

Elliot stopped and slouched. "What?" he groaned. He didn't look back.

"I'm off next day so I wanted to wish you a Merry Christmas in case I don't see you again beforehand."

Just the words "Merry Christmas" dug under Elliot's skin. "What do you got to be merry about, kid? We're all gonna die someday." He pushed the door open to leave.

The new guy mumbled, "Jesus. Who pissed in your oatmeal, Scrooge?"

Elliot paused in the doorway. *Scrooge?* Now, that was funny. He glanced back with a grunt and then walked out. Before the door swung shut, he shouted, "Humbug." What followed was the closest he'd get to a chuckle.

For the next hour he stood alone in the bay, staring out the back window at the parking lot. Next to the window was a glass display case holding a set of fire gear and a helmet. The plaque at the bottom memorialized some firefighter named Ted who died in the line of duty in 1995, before Elliot got on the department. He was still waiting to see a display made for Jimmy, though he knew there wouldn't be one. Firefighters didn't like to be reminded of what can happen if the job got to be too much for them.

He barely listened to the lieutenant's change-of-shift report before heading to his truck. He figured Boy Scout Carl would pass along any pertinent information that the oncoming medic crew might need to know, like the oxygen tank level or what needed replacing in the med kit.

Elliot nearly fell asleep twice on his half-hour drive

home, the spaced lines between lanes melding together in a hypnotic blur. The snow was starting to stick to the road and he got slowed by a salt truck taking up a lane and a half. "Idiot," he shouted once he finally got around it.

He spent most of his two days off staring at vapid TV shows and interacting with his wife and ten-year-old daughter as little as possible. They didn't understand how miserable he was and selfishly wanted him to snap out of it. He just wanted to be left alone with a nice glass of Evan Williams bourbon and a Coke.

When Elliot's alarm clock rang for him to wake for his Christmas Eve shift following three hours of interrupted sleep, he considered throwing it through the wall. He was careful not to wake his wife, Chloe, as he got ready and left for work. She wasn't speaking to him, anyway—the result of yet another argument the night before.

On his way to work, he stopped at a gas station for some coffee. The clerk wore an obnoxious red and green holiday sweater that had a reindeer with flappy ears on the front. She said, "Have a merry Christmas," with a toothy smile and Elliot could have strangled the cheerfulness out of her.

He was a few miles away before he took his first sip. The coffee was old and the cream smelled slightly curdled. "Are you effing kidding me?" He cracked his window and tossed the coffee out, cup and all.

Elliot pulled into Station 22's parking lot with two minutes to spare before roll call. He didn't speak to anyone as he awaited his truck assignment for the day. Medic 22.

As always.

He slogged through the first half of his twenty-four-hour shift, aiming for minimal conversations with the others in the crew, especially Carl. A quiet day was a good day. If he heard one more comment in passing about how lucky they were to have such a white Christmas, he thought he might vomit.

Lunch was a potluck to celebrate the holidays with the firefighters' families invited. Since Elliot hadn't brought anything or invited his own family, he steered clear of the kitchen until the husbands and wives and kids had left. Then he sneaked in and made himself a plate of leftovers that he ate alone in the dingy basement of the sixty-year-old station. The occasional loud snap and hiss of the air compressor reminded him of why he didn't just stay in the basement all day. That and the spiders.

He made his bunk around 9:30 and brushed his teeth. The rest of the crew, all seven other firefighters minus the two lieutenants who had already retired to their private rooms, hooted it up in the kitchen. Elliot was glad to miss the juvenile ribbings and stale jokes. There was a time when he might have been the ringleader, but that was before.

While lying in bed, he imagined the scene. Elliot had heard all their jokes before. The only one witty enough to make him laugh on occasion was Greg. He liked Greg best. The others were probably making fun of the way Greg was always eating yet never gained any weight, calling him Tapeworm. Again. For the thousandth time. Or maybe they were hacking on Lauren, who gave as good as she got, or mocking Charlie's nervous habit of clearing his throat every few minutes. Sal was surely the only one sitting quietly at the end of the table. He usually just took in the nonsense with his stoic face. He had earned the nickname Fun-sucker because he was often serious to a fault.

Elliot crawled into bed just as happy to be alone as he would be to fake nice with the jokesters. More so, actually. As he lay his head on the pillow, he hoped not to have any Gladyses for one night. He could use a few solid hours of sleep.

One by one, the rest of the crew entered the bunk room, made their beds, and lay down. It was 11:30 before Elliot's brain slowed enough to go to sleep.

It could have been a half-hour or two days later when his metal locker banged like someone had struck it with an open hand. He sprang out of bed. "What?" he snapped as he focused in the darkness. There was no one there.

Sal groaned from his corner bunk, "Keep it down, Elliot."

Elliot gave him the finger even though Sal didn't actually open his eyes. He lay back down and pulled the covers up to his neck. The other firefighters kept it so freezing in the bunkroom that he could almost see his breath. Whoever heard of running air conditioners in the winter? The clock read 12:00. His weighted eyelids slowly closed again. But before he could drift back to sleep, a slight breeze whistled between the lockers and wafted across his neck. He shivered and pulled the covers tighter. The tail end of the breeze carried a whisper that moaned, "Elllliiiooot."

Elliot sat up with a start. "Who said that?" It was probably one of the ladder jerks playing a prank. "Greg? Was that you?"

Greg rolled over and continued snoring. Carl's sleep apnea machine buzzed at the other end of the room.

The moonlight shining through the windows highlighted the sleeping firefighters. None of the windows were open, yet the breeze returned and grew into a steady wind that caught the double doors leading to the apparatus bay and tossed them open, only to slam them shut again. Even that didn't wake any of the others. Elliot wished he could sleep so soundly.

He lay motionless on his side, hoping to go back to sleep. The covers were tugged from his shoulders like someone had pulled at them. He yanked them back up. And then something nudged his lower back. He wrenched his head around, but no one was there. He licked his dry lips. Maybe a drink would calm his nerves. He climbed from his bed and pulled his uniform pants over his shorts. Still in his socks, he marched through the bunkroom and into the bay.

He stood behind the ladder truck, his head a couple of feet below the bucket that extended from the back. He hated working from inside that bucket, mostly because he didn't like heights.

Something clanked. He cocked his head.

"Is someone in there?" he called out.

The apparatus bay was quiet.

Eerily quiet.

Elliot sighed. "You're going crazy," he mumbled to himself. He reached for the doors to go back to bed, deciding against a glass of water. When his hand met the handle, a new sound rattled along the opposite side of the medic truck near the kitchen. He hesitated. It sounded like empty bottles being dragged across the floor. Elliot's hand hovered over the handle. "Greg?" he called out. "Are you eating again?"

The dim fluorescent lights of the apparatus bay

suddenly flared to life, blazing like the sun at high noon, every one of them audibly buzzing with energy. He squinted to focus.

Though the buzzing sound was faint at first, it quickly grew into a throaty rumble. The fluorescent lights swelled into overfilled balloons, bulging with brilliance and straining not to pop. They were too blinding to look at and Elliot had to shade his eyes with one hand. Once they reached their limits, they quivered and then burst with a single concussive boom. Raining glass battered the bucket and the floor. Darkness washed through the bay like a tsunami of the blackest ink. It stole his breath and nearly stopped his heart.

He stood alone, trying to straighten his brain over what he had just witnessed. He expected some of his coworkers to stumble from the bunkroom to investigate, but the double doors remained shut.

Silence.

Loneliness.

Death.

And then a bluish glow brightened the wall above the medic truck as the clinking bottles moved toward the front. Elliot leaned down, expecting to see a pair of work boots in the glow from the other side. No one was there.

Wind howled through the bay, whispering his name again.

"Hello?" he asked timidly.

A man awash in the strange blue light floated around the front of the medic truck wearing a long, tattered robe that danced softly behind him. He dragged his jagged fingers along the overhead door. They were glassy like icicles hanging from a gutter. The stranger drifted toward him with the fluidity of a calm morning wave on the beach. A half-dozen empty whisky bottles tied to ropes rattled over the concrete floor behind him. They must have been heavy judging by the way they seemed to tug the man's shoulders backward.

Though Elliot wanted to retreat, his legs wouldn't work. He regarded the stranger from his bony bare feet to his tattered robe and settled on his pale, ghostly face within the blue glow. The stranger's lower jaw was missing, leaving a deep hole that Elliot momentarily lost himself in. A thousand tiny tortured souls writhed and moaned and called out his name from within the cavern beneath the man's nose.

Elliot dragged his eyes away from the mesmerizing pit and up to the man's eyes. The stranger fixed him with a deathly vacant gaze. Something about him seemed familiar, like a distant friend Elliot hadn't seen since elementary school. Elliot summoned the courage to speak. "Who are you?" he asked.

The familiar stranger tilted his head. A worm slithered from one of his eyes before disappearing inside the other. His lost gaze narrowed to study Elliot's face. Something fell from the hole where his mouth should have been and pinged off the floor. Elliot followed it with his eyes. It was a nubby piece of metal about the size of a BB.

The stranger reached down, picked it up, and stuffed it back into his face. "You don't recognize me?" he asked, despite not having a jaw.

Elliot's eyes widened and he swallowed acid. He'd recognize that hoarse voice anywhere. "Jimmy?"

Jimmy looked more tired than he ever had in life and his shoulders slouched like the weight of the whisky bottles was too much to carry. "I haven't heard that name in years." He looked around. "The station hasn't changed much, has it?"

Elliot's heart skipped. "Oh my god, Jimmy." He fought back tears. "You selfish bastard. I can't believe what you did." If he wasn't so terrified, he'd punch his old friend. "Why did you do it?"

Jimmy looked to the ceiling for a moment. Then he lowered his eyes again. "I don't wanna talk about that."

"Wrong answer. You left me here. You were the one rock in my life who understood what we go through in this job. Chloe tried, but she can't. I hate you for what you did. Every day … Every goddamn day for the last seven years, I've tortured myself, knowing that there was something more I could have done. What did you need from me?" His first tear since Jimmy's funeral touched his cheek.

Jimmy's eyes saddened and he tilted his head. "What happened to me wasn't about you, Elliot. There was nothing you could have done."

It must be a dream. Elliot slapped his own cheek to wake up.

"You're not dreaming, my old friend."

"Then why are you here?"

"I'm a guide." The empty bottles pulled at Jimmy's back and he gave them an annoyed tug. "This'll be you if you don't pay close attention on tonight's adventure."

"Adventure? I can't go anywhere. You know that. I'm working."

Jimmy rolled his dead eyes. "A job you despise, just like I did at the end."

Elliot scoffed. "You were weak. You took the easy way out. And you left the rest of us here to pick up the pieces."

"Haven't you considered doing the same?"

"Well, yeah. But …"

"Don't you already have a plan?"

Elliot turned away. Sadness was easier to manage by smothering it with anger, and that's what he did.

"I know what you're planning, Elliot. I've seen the gun in your bedside table. I've seen you hold it to your head."

"Fuck you, Jimmy. I'm not talking about this with you. You're the last person who can lecture me about this."

Jimmy shrugged his shoulders and pitched a skeptical glower at him. "This is your final opportunity to avoid sharing my personal hell. After tonight, what you choose to do is your business. I won't have anything else to say on the matter."

Elliot shook his head. "I'm not interested in whatever you're offering. I'm doing fine."

"Are you, now?" Jimmy's face contorted angrily. "Oh, my foolish friend." Suddenly, he shot forward, his face stopping inches from Elliot's. His cheekbones pressed through his decaying flesh and worms crawled frantically over the tiny tortured souls within the gaping hole. He roared, "DO YOU WANT TO END UP LIKE MEEEEEE?" The walls shook and his face melted.

Then he settled back and took a calming breath through his nose. Elliot couldn't speak.

Jimmy broke the long silence. "You will be haunted by three ghosts tonight, Elliot. One on every even hour. You don't get to choose whether you go on this journey, but you can choose whether or not you pay attention before it's too late."

"Ghosts? Jimmy, do you know how insane this is?"

Jimmy shrugged. "This is your last chance." He turned and dragged his bottles toward the closed overhead bay door, hesitating when he got there. He glanced back and then lowered his head. "Good luck, Elliot." He passed through the door like light through a window.

Elliot wasn't ready for Jimmy to leave just yet. He had too many questions. He raced to catch up. His nose flattened painfully against the metal door and he stumbled backward.

"Jimmy?" he whispered. Then he gritted his teeth. "This is stupid. Ghosts. Right." He marched back to bed. He wasn't going anywhere, ghosts or no ghosts.

STAVE TWO
CHRISTMAS PAST

Elliot's eyes shot open and he scrambled to see the clock. He held his breath. It was 2:00 on the button. He sighed. With a smirk, he rolled over. *Three ghosts. Yeah, right.* How dumb was he to even entertain such a crazy dream? After pulling his blanket over his shoulders, he closed his eyes again.

Before he fell back to sleep, the overhead PA crackled to life with the static that typically preceded an alarm. *Damn it.* The long, steady tone that announced fires followed. Usually, the fire tones sent the firefighters in a mad rush to the trucks, but none of the others moved. Instead of the familiar computerized dispatcher reporting an alarm, Jimmy's deep and menacing voice said, "It's time, Elliot."

Are you shitting me? "I don't wanna go," Elliot answered.

A strange throbbing warmth met his back as the mattress grew hotter and hotter like a stove burner. He shifted and squirmed, but it kept getting more and more uncomfortable. When he couldn't stand the heat any longer, he sprang from the bunk and stood with his arms crossed at the foot of his bed. "I'm still not going."

The PA sighed. Then Jimmy answered, "We're on a schedule here, Elliot."

Elliot scanned the room. "Hey, guys," he shouted. "Wake up." He shook Sal's bunk, but Sal didn't even stir. Then he shook Carl's bunk, also to no avail. He considered ripping off Carl's apnea mask, but decided against it.

"Are we finished messing around?" Jimmy asked over the PA.

An invisible hand grabbed Elliot's shirt collar and yanked him to his rear. He clawed at the hand as it dragged him helplessly through the bunkroom toward the doors.

"Get up," he screamed to the other firefighters as he passed. "Help me." The invisible hand on his collar yanked him through the doors, past the stupid Christmas tree that sparkled in the dark with its winding string of colored lights, and off the ground toward the ladder bucket. The bucket's door creaked open and the invisible hand tossed him inside. The door slammed closed. He jerked his collar straight, stood up, and dusted himself off.

As he stood petrified in the dark, a tiny, glowing, orange ember floated past his face, bright and beautiful in the blackness. He wanted to touch it. A trail of wispy smoke highlighted by the ember's dull glow followed it to the floor, tiny flares of orange pulsating. He looked around, but nothing was burning that he could see. He reached for the door latch just as the truck's engine coughed to life and the bucket shrugged. At the other end of the ladder, the cab belched and seized before the bucket shimmied and lurched upward. Elliot grabbed one of the handles and squeezed like it was his lifeline.

The bucket shot toward the ceiling, gaining speed as it climbed. Elliot covered his head and squatted below the bucket's rim. Like an explosive birth, the bucket crashed through the ceiling, raining pieces of concrete and wood around him and onto the floor below. He squeezed his eyes shut and gripped the inside handle with both hands.

The bucket raced toward the heavens with the speed of a rocket. Elliot pleaded, "Please stop. Please stop. Please stop," but whoever controlled the ladder ignored him. He pried his eyes open against the wind's velocity and his own fear as he headed for the clouds. His cheeks flapped in the pounding gale. The air thinned and a cold mist surrounded him before the bucket jolted to a violent stop, almost flinging him out. Thankfully, he had a strong grip. The bucket bounced and jostled for a few nerve-wracking seconds before it settled.

Elliot found himself curled on the bucket floor, chunks of the concrete roof surrounding him. His next breath left him in a quivering mist, floating like a puff of baby powder. His hands trembled. The sudden chaos bled into quiet calm as the bucket started moving again and eased into the clouds.

With one hand around the handle, he pulled himself to his knees before finding enough strength in his legs to stand up.

Though he begged himself not to look over the side, curiosity pushed him toward the waist-high wall. He cautiously leaned his head over, his grip still strangling the handle. His stomach dropped like he'd unexpectedly driven over a dip in the road. His daughter called that the tickles.

The ladder stretched from the bucket, through the clouds, and out of sight to the city below. The downtown lights of Columbus, Ohio blazed in the north like a photo from a satellite. Elliot backed up to the center again, his every movement amplified by the nauseating sway of the bucket. He grabbed one of the three joysticks that controlled the ladder and pulled the one that retracted it. The bucket hiccupped, but didn't move. He yanked the lowering joystick with the same result. He was stuck. His only choice was a sickening one. He would have to climb down. If the normal one-hundred-foot climb of the fully extended ladder was enough to give him the creeps, this one was enough to stop his heart. Walking on the wing of a plane might have been less terrifying.

He inhaled a deep breath and grabbed the rails of the ladder that rounded downward to meet the top of the bucket. Before he could climb out, he noticed a fiery orange glow sailing up toward him. As the flames neared the top, Elliot saw a figure at the center, its feet never touching the rungs. The burning figure moved with a fluidity that held Elliot's gaze. As it got even closer, Elliot realized it was a woman.

Elliot's back met the opposite wall of the bucket near the controls. The burning woman hovered above the ladder like a cloud. Being on fire didn't appear to trouble her. Ashes lifted from her face and crumbled into nothingness. She tilted her head and floated into the bucket beside him. She was beautiful. Hypnotizing.

Elliot shielded his face despite not feeling any heat. "What do you want with me?" he asked.

She shot closer and clutched Elliot's shirt like a bully shaking down a schoolmate for lunch money. Her long, scarlet hair seemed to flow in slow motion, images of Elliot's life playing across each strand. It was like watching movies on a pin head and he was stunned that he could even make out the images. He caught a brief flash of his daughter's smile as one strand danced past his eyes. It was from when she was six and starting ballet lessons. She'd looked like a flower in her new leotard and ballet skirt. He'd started calling her his little Tulip and the nickname had stuck. Another strand showed his dad, young and shirtless, mowing the lawn of his childhood home. And yet another revealed his wife sitting at a bar the night he'd finally gathered the stones to go over and say hi. He was mesmerized.

A slight smile crossed the ghost's lips. "I am the ghost of Christmas Past. I have much to show you and little time to do it." Her voice echoed around him as if it came from everywhere but her mouth. She released his shirt.

"What do you want from me?" he asked.

She shoved Elliot aside and took the ladder controls. "You'll soon see. Now, hold on." She jammed the lowering joystick down and the bucket dropped like it had detached from the ladder. Elliot's feet lifted off the floor and he pulled on the handle to hold himself down. The wind howled, brightening the ghost's flames to a blinding magnificence. His lips quivered like Jell-O on a rollercoaster. Despite the whipping winds, Christmas Past's hair continued to float gently around her.

The bucket finally screeched to a halt, throwing him against the side and then back to the floor.

The ghost extended her hand. "We're here. Get up, please."

Elliot swatted her hand away and got up on his own. He rubbed his sore shoulder. The novelty of these ghosts was wearing thin fast. "So, where are we?" he grumbled.

Christmas Past stepped aside and gestured to the ladder controls. "See for yourself."

Elliot balked.

She gestured again. "Go on."

He reached for the joysticks and looked over the rim. The long, flat roof of a business with a packed parking lot sat just beneath the bucket. He smelled barbeque and subconsciously licked his lips. He was a sucker for ribs.

The joystick was touchy and his first tugs caused the bucket to hiccup until he got the hang of it. He gently nudged the joystick toward the roof. Once he reached the top and stopped, she motioned for him to keep going. The bucket slowly passed through the roof.

Inside was a packed restaurant with waiters and busboys scurrying around a full house. People walked directly below them without looking up. Elliot looked to Christmas Past, confused.

"They don't see us, do they?" he asked, though the answer was obvious.

She shook her head.

"And they can't hear us, either?"

She shook her head again.

People ate and talked and laughed. A row of TVs played college football games above the bar. A cheery hostess stood near the front, asking patrons to donate money or gifts for less fortunate children to put under the Christmas tree behind her.

Elliot shrugged. "Okay. I give up. What am I looking for in here?"

Christmas Past gestured toward a specific table behind him. Elliot followed her eyes to a young couple holding hands in a booth. His mouth gaped. He staggered. "Is that …? How?"

"Get us closer. Don't you want to hear what you're saying?"

As real as he was standing in the ladder bucket, he

was looking at himself and Chloe. They were only babies. Hell, he still had bangs. He mumbled, "How old am I? Early twenties? We aren't even married yet."

She answered, "Twenty-one years, three months, and two days. Do you remember what you were doing here?"

Elliot shook his head. He'd eaten at that rib joint many times.

"Go closer and listen."

Elliot extended the bucket through several oblivious waiters and stopped next to the booth. He eyed his smiling younger self who was giddily ignorant of how the world really was.

"Ma'am?" his younger self called to a server who wore pink lipstick.

She passed through the bucket and stopped to lean on the table. "Whatcha need, hon?"

"We're splurging tonight. Do you have strawberry daiquiris?"

"We do."

"We'll take two."

She carded him and Chloe.

Elliot's memory rushed back. He shook his head. Imagine being so young and sheltered that strawberry daiquiris counted as splurging. He grabbed the joystick. "Okay, I don't need to see anymore. I know what you're doing, and it won't work." He yanked the controls, but the bucket didn't move.

"What are you celebrating?" the server asked.

The naïve younger Elliot smiled like a doofus. "You are looking at the newest Columbus firefighter. They offered me a job today."

"Well, isn't that amazing? Congratulations."

What a buffoon.

"Thank you," young Elliot answered.

"When do you start?" she asked.

"Next week."

"That sounds exciting. Good luck. And be careful. I imagine it's a pretty dangerous job." With that, she excused herself and headed to the bar for their drinks.

Young Elliot turned to Chloe. "You know what this means, don't you?"

She turned to him with concern heavy in her eyes. As a young man, Elliot had been too excited to notice, but it was so obvious seeing her now. She said, "That I'm never going to sleep well while you're at work?"

"No, babe. It means my career is set. We don't have to worry about insurance, or retirement, or where next week's paycheck will come from. We can start a family."

She grinned. "I'm so proud of you."

"This is the second greatest day of my life."

She tilted her head. "Oh? And what's the first?"

Elliot mouthed his younger self's words. "The day I met you."

In typical Chloe fashion, she rolled her eyes and answered, "You're so cheesy."

In the bucket, Elliot turned his back as the waiter returned with the drinks. "So, what now? I'm supposed to suddenly forget everything I've seen and done on the job because you showed me a vision of when I was a dumb kid?" He spun back and leaned toward the happy young couple. "Hey, dumbass. Enjoy life now. It only goes in the shitter later."

Christmas Past shook her head.

Elliot scowled at her. "I get it. Can we go now?"

Christmas Past sadly nodded.

Without looking at his younger self again, Elliot pulled the joystick. The bucket blasted through the ceiling and into the brisk night. Christmas Past's flames led the way. The bucket swooped and swayed and rode the wind through the city streets. Elliot leaned over the edge to watch the ground whip by. Part of him wanted to jump out and be done with it altogether, and part of him wanted to finish his shift so he could get home to a nice cold drink.

The bucket stayed near the ground as it followed the road through 22's district and past the station. Elliot recognized the old white Dodge truck he'd owned fifteen or so years ago driving away as other off-duty firefighters walked through the parking lot to their cars. The bucket followed his truck down the street, slowly gaining on it. Elliot watched curiously.

The bucket moved close enough that he could see himself driving. He still had a full head of hair like in the last vision. His younger self's tired, drooping eyes drifted from the road. His head bobbed and then jerked back up, his eyes wide open. He rubbed them and shook his head. Then he cracked the window in hopes the brisk air would wake him up a bit.

Christmas Past leaned in and whispered, "You went home from work pretty tired a lot of times, huh?"

Elliot nodded. "Yeah. Probably another busy day and night on the medic."

She tilted her head. "I suspect so."

"What's this have to do with anything?"

"Just watch."

Young Elliot's head bobbed again, but this time he didn't startle himself awake. The truck coasted toward the center line.

Elliot muttered, "Wake up, idiot." He looked ahead to where a green traffic light clicked to yellow and then to red. His eyes widened and he looked into his old truck again. His younger self still slept with his head bowed. Caught in the moment, Elliot forgot the past part of Christmas Past and panicked. "Look out," he screamed.

There was a car waiting in the perpendicular lane, oblivious to young Elliot's approach. Time slowed for everyone but Elliot and Christmas Past.

She throttled the bucket forward, moving ahead of Elliot's truck and toward the other car as that lane's traffic light flipped to green. The driver gave it a little gas. He still didn't see Elliot's truck coming. The bucket carried Elliot into the other car's back seat. An older man was driving with an older woman sitting in the passenger seat where the brunt of the impact was about to happen. They approached the intersection to start their left turn.

The passenger casually looked to her right and then screamed, "Harold. Look out." She tensed up and drew her arms across her face.

The older man stomped on the brakes barely in time for Elliot's truck to barrel through the intersection inches from his front bumper. Harold lay on the horn. The long, melting blare of the horn matched the slowing down of everything around them.

Elliot looked through the windshield and into his old truck's driver's side window as his younger self jerked his head up and grabbed the wheel. Stunned, his idiot younger self looked around, oblivious to the destruction he had almost caused. Then he continued down the road as if nothing had happened.

Harold took a calming breath. His hand was draped across his passenger's chest as if he could have held her back like a seatbelt had they crashed. He slowly withdrew his shaky arm. He said, "Are you all right,

Gladys?"

Elliot's face twisted. "Why's that name sound so familiar?" he asked.

Christmas Past grinned.

His shoulders tensed. "Oh, right. The old lady who called us out in the middle of the night for her stupid blood pressure. I remember."

"You don't feel anything knowing she saved your life here?"

Elliot bristled. "Well, she saved herself as much as she saved me."

"If that's what you believe."

"Are we finished yet?" he said with disdain.

She shook her head.

The bucket lifted through the roof of the car and stretched toward the outer edge of his district. He knew it well.

The sun peeked over the horizon. Medic 22 and Engine 22 were parked in front of an apartment building with their emergency lights on. They took a lot of calls to that complex.

Christmas Past touched Elliot's shoulder. "Do you remember this?"

He scoffed at the notion that he'd remember one call out of thousands and shook his head.

"Let's go in and have a look."

The bucket carried them through the main door and into apartment C. An older lady was standing beside the door crying. Elliot's old crew was scrambling around a man lying on his back on the floor. He was pale, his lifeless eyes were open, and his mouth was agape. His body jerked with each thrust of Sal's hands on his chest. Lauren held a mask over the man's face and squeezed the bag every few seconds. A tube ran from the mask to an oxygen bottle. The

29

man's cheeks puffed out with each forced breath.

Elliot saw himself squatting over the man's head. This version still had some hair up top, though it was getting thin.

Greg attached the cardiac monitor to the man's chest.

Christmas Past asked, "Do you remember now?"

Elliot shook his head again. "I've done this a lot over the years."

Young Elliot shouted, "Give him a milligram of epi as soon as you get that IV."

A young, healthy Jimmy was there too. He lifted his attention from the older man's left arm. A used IV needle lay on the carpet. "I didn't get it."

The younger Elliot answered, "Give him an IO."

Christmas Past leaned toward Elliot's ear. "May I ask, what is an IO?"

"It's like an IV, but we drill a needle into the bone instead of putting one in the vein."

"Ahhh. And that works?"

"Yep."

Jimmy grabbed the IO drill, but hesitated.

Elliot whispered, "Oh. I remember this now. Jimmy had never done one on a real person before. IOs were pretty new at the time." He leaned over the rim of the bucket and shouted, "I'm picking up your slack just like old times, huh, buddy?" He settled back into the bucket with a haughty grin. "Watch this."

Jimmy held out the drill in hopes Elliot would take over. Elliot snatched it. Before he shoved the drill against the man's shoulder, he told Jimmy to pay attention and then described right where to place it.

Once the needle was drilled into the old man's shoulder, Jimmy pushed the epinephrine through the line. "Epi's in," he said.

Younger Elliot was a whirlwind, managing the cardiac arrest and barking orders to the others.

Elliot looked back to Christmas Past. "I was pretty good, huh?" He bounced his eyebrows.

She smiled. "That you were. What about now?"

He shrugged and his grin faded. "Eh. You gotta give a shit to be good at this job."

While reading the monitor, his younger self paused for a second and lifted his eyes and looked directly at the bucket. What could only be described as disappointment washed over his face. Elliot locked eyes with him for a fleeting moment and his chest fluttered. Then his younger self shook it away and dove back into his work. "V-fib. Let's give him a shock."

Greg pushed a button on the monitor and then ordered everyone to stand clear. Once the monitor charged fully and everyone had removed their hands from the old man, he pushed another button and electricity jolted the man's entire body. The lady near the door gasped and sobbed louder.

Everyone waited to see if the shock changed the rhythm. Even Christmas Past leaned forward slightly.

Lauren shouted, "I have a pulse, guys."

Younger Elliot said, "Load him up. I'll get his information and meet you in the truck." He rushed over to the older lady.

Christmas Past whispered, "This is the part I like."

Elliot didn't remember what came next and watched like it was a movie.

"Ma'am," his younger self asked, "what's your name?"

Elliot didn't recognize his own voice.

Christmas Past leaned in. "That's how you sound

when you're being sympathetic."

Elliot scoffed.

The older lady's voice was shaky. "Martha."

Younger Elliot answered, "All right, Martha. Your husband's still very sick, but we were able to get his pulse back. We're going to take him to the hospital. You can ride with us in the front seat if you'd like."

Her eyes flooded with equal sadness and hope. She buried her face in his chest. "Thank you," she cried.

Without hesitation, he put his hand on her back and lightly rubbed. He whispered, "You have to be strong, Martha. We're going to do everything we can to help him, okay?"

She leaned back and looked into his eyes. "I don't know what we would do without people like you."

When the crew carried the old man past, Martha touched her husband's hand. "Keep fighting, Frank. I'll be at the hospital when you wake up."

Younger Elliot smiled. "Martha, I need some information."

In the bucket, Elliot rubbed the back of his neck. "There. I wasn't always a prick. Are you happy?"

Christmas Past shrugged. "This isn't about me."

"Well, like I said. You gotta give a shit, and I'm fresh out."

"So you keep saying. Go ahead. Take us out of here."

Elliot grabbed the controls and started to lift the bucket, but stopped.

"What is it?" Christmas Past asked.

Elliot looked to his hands and picked at the rubber casing around the joystick. He mumbled, "Did he live?"

"What's that?"

He asked again a little louder.

"Well, Elliot, I'm happy to inform you that he did live. He was able to spend seven more wonderful years with Martha."

"But he's dead now, though, right?"

"Well, everybody dies someday."

"So, what good did I do in the grand scheme of things?"

"I can't answer that for you."

He crossed his arms. "Are we done?"

She shook her head. Her hair floated past his eyes with another moment in time flashing across the strands. It was Chloe sitting on a Fort Myers beach in Florida. He knew it was Fort Myers because that was their favorite place to go. She looked back with a sultry glance and bit her pouty lower lip. He noticed her small baby bump and remembered how proud she was of it. And then, just as quickly, the strand was gone again. He wanted to see more.

"I have one more thing to show you, Elliot, but I need you to prepare yourself for this one. It'll be difficult to see."

"Oh, great. I can't wait."

She ignored his sarcasm. "Lift us up, then."

He eased the joystick forward and the bucket carried them through the ceiling. It was a gorgeous afternoon, a bit chilly with not a cloud in the sky and no Christmas decorations in sight. They were above a freeway with stopped cars backed up for miles.

A sick feeling grew in the back of his mind. As they continued past the stopped cars, Elliot's eyes widened and he realized where they were headed. He shook his head. "Oh no. I'm not doing this anymore." His voice lifted in volume. "Take me back to the station."

"I'm sorry, Elliot. You must see this."

Tears welled up in his eyes. The thought of what was ahead was too much to take. "This isn't fair. I'm not doing it. I refuse." He tried to stop the bucket, but it continued speeding over the line of stopped cars. Some of the drivers stuck their heads out of their windows to see what was holding them up.

Angry and desperate, Elliot searched the bucket for something to stop the vision. He found an extinguisher, pulled the pin, and aimed the nozzle at Christmas Past's flaming head. With his eyes closed, he squeezed the handle. A blizzard of snowy chemicals engulfed her. He emptied the entire extinguisher before he took another breath. He lowered it to his side.

She waved her hand in front of her face until the chemicals dissipated. "Are you quite finished?" she asked. Her flames appeared even more brilliant than before.

He tossed the extinguisher aside and clenched his fists in front of his chest until they quivered in frustration. "Damn you," he shouted.

She stared back, emotionless.

He wanted to punch something, but all that was nearby was the control panel. He instantly regretted it the moment his knuckles smashed against it.

"Do you feel better?" she asked.

He closed his eyes and bowed his head. He took a deep, calming breath and let it out slowly. It wasn't her that he should be mad at. Resigned, he nodded a single time.

The bucket approached a semi-truck with a smashed front end and its trailer jackknifed across the road. About twenty yards in front of it, an SUV sat cockeyed with its crumpled rear bumper where the back seat should have been. Medic 22 and Engine 22 were already on the scene. A Rescue truck rode the berm alongside the line of traffic. Several police cruisers were parked all over the grassy median. Police officers stood in the path of the bucket holding white sheets up like curtains.

"Why are they doing that?" Christmas Past asked.

"So everyone else doesn't see the little girl."

"Oh."

Elliot's tears threatened to spill even before the bucket passed through the makeshift curtains. On the other side was a special kind of controlled chaos that firefighters learned to live within. Sal raced to the medic truck for more supplies while Carl looked for a vein for an IV on a skinny little arm that lay limply by his knee.

The younger Elliot knelt over the sweet, innocent face of a seven-year-old girl. She was unconscious. To look at her face, one would think she was merely gazing at the sky, daydreaming. Most of her injuries were internal except for her lower leg twisted into an S-shape and her unnaturally pointing foot.

"Hold on, Katie," the younger Elliot cried. "We're going to help you."

While Elliot and the crew worked, Katie's parents knelt beside him and whispered prayers throughout the ordeal. They never faltered.

In the bucket, Christmas Past touched Elliot's shoulder. "This is the moment when it happened, huh?"

The tears were flowing down his cheeks. His gut twisted. Someone stabbed him repeatedly from inside his chest. He nodded. He watched the person he used to be pause and drop to his heels. His shoulders slumped. A medical helicopter circled overhead.

"What did you see just then?" Christmas Past

asked.

Elliot stared from the bucket, a tourniquet cutting off his words.

"Elliot, what did you see?"

He bowed his head and stuttered in a breath. He didn't want to answer.

"It's time you face what broke you."

"I can't."

"You have to. Tell me what you saw."

His voice wobbled as he answered, "I saw the life leave her."

"What do you mean?"

"I saw whatever made Katie Katie leave her. Sometimes when it happens, you just know."

"But you were still trying to save her. Tell me how you were so sure she would die."

"It was in her eyes. I don't know if she could see me, but I felt like she was begging me for help. And then, at that moment, she wasn't begging anymore. Whatever we did from that moment on was pointless. I'd heard that the eyes are the windows to our souls, but I never fully understood what that meant until then. When I close my eyes at night, when I look at my daughter, I see Katie. She was looking to me—her last hope—and I failed her. When her eyes went blank, my heart died too, I guess."

"But you didn't fail her. There was nothing more you could do."

He bowed his head. "Yeah. That's what they say." After a few seconds, he looked at his past self who was struggling to place a tube down Katie's throat. He whispered, "I'm so sorry, Riley. I wish I could have helped you."

"Elliot, that's not your daughter lying there."

Elliot put his hands over his face. "I meant Katie."

Without the anger, he had nothing but emptiness inside. One of the police officers holding the sheets wiped her eyes. If only Jimmy had still been there to talk with after. Why did that bastard have to leave? Elliot watched himself help carry the stretcher to the medical helicopter that had landed on the median. When the helicopter lifted into the air, Elliot remembered feeling that nothing would ever be the same again. It was an awful, helpless feeling. He remembered the blackness of anger and helplessness creeping in and replacing the hope and wonder that had once lived in his soul. Maybe it was a coping mechanism. Or maybe it was years of seeing people die. Either way, it was all he had to keep warm.

Christmas Past caressed his back. Her touch was warm and soothing. Elliot broke down and cried as hard as he had ever cried. "It wasn't fair," he blubbered through his fingers. "Kids shouldn't suffer like that."

The pain was too crushing, so Elliot did what he had done every day of the three years since. He swallowed hard and turned the sadness into anger again. He spun and lunged toward Christmas Past, stopping with his face inches from hers. Compassion filled her fiery gaze. His face twisted in rage. "Why?" he screamed. "Why do I have to live through this again? You don't think I live it every day of my goddamn life?"

"You live it because you need to understand that it wasn't your fault."

Elliot whipped back around and glowered hatefully at the medic truck that had brought him all his pain. "And what good does that do her?" He sighed. "I don't want to see any more. Please, just take me home."

The bucket jostled him slightly before slowly pulling up and away from the scene as his past self stood hopeless in the middle of the freeway among a sea of bloody trauma dressings and discarded medical wrappers. It was just like he'd said: Katie wasn't the only one who'd died that day.

Soon, the crash scene faded below and returned to that special, secret place in his mind where the morbid movie theater relentlessly played on. When the bucket stopped, Elliot lifted his eyes to Christmas Past. Her flames were muted and her face glowed with strange optimism. "Elliot, I must tell you one more thing before I leave you."

"I can't take any more."

"You must hear this. Because of you and your crew, Katie held on in the hospital for two more days. She had family out of town who were able to make it back in time to say goodbye. Because of what you did and what you do, Katie's organs saved the lives of four other people."

Elliot scoffed. "I don't care about them. I just wanted to save her. I know what you're trying to do, and I appreciate it. But I'm fine. I'll get by like I always have."

The corners of her mouth drooped downward. "Then you have not learned from my visit and I am sorry. Goodbye, Elliot." She unceremoniously pushed him out of the bucket.

Elliot rocketed toward Earth. He frantically grasped at the air, but there was nothing to stop his fall. He squeezed his eyes closed. An instant before he hit the ground, he jerked awake in his bed gasping for air, sweat pouring from his face and sticking his shirt to his back. He sat up, clutching his chest. Then he pulled his knees up and rocked back and forth.

Sal walked past from the bathroom. He scratched his ass and belched. "Bad dream?" he asked. Then he crawled back into bed.

Elliot didn't answer. The clock caught his eye.

3:59.

It clicked to 4:00.

The PA crackled.

STAVE THREE
CHRISTMAS PRESENT

Elliot glared at the buzzing PA speaker. "I know, I know. I'm going."

Jimmy's voice sounded eager when he said, "Don't be late."

Elliot wearily climbed out of bed and slogged through the double doors into the apparatus bay. He wondered what new surprises awaited him. He rubbed his arms, the briskness settling in a touch more than it had before. As he passed the Christmas tree, he unplugged it. *Enough holiday cheer for one night.*

The shattered bay lights were whole and working again. Elliot looked up to the ladder bucket. It was empty. He stepped around the back of the ladder where he could see Engine 22. Someone stood beside the pump panel pulling on levers and twisting knobs as if he knew what he was doing. He obviously didn't.

"Hey," Elliot shouted.

The stranger turned with a start. He was a plump man fully encased in a cocoon of gushing water. Only his face was free, swollen and pale with blueish lips and bulging eyes. Elliot had seen enough bloated bodies pulled from a nearby river to not be too shocked.

Oh," the ghost gasped. "I didn't hear you coming."

He glanced back at the pump panel. "This is confusing. How do you know what switches to flip when?"

"It's not difficult." Elliot found himself starting to explain and stopped.

The ghost's beard was a waterfall that splashed the floor, the drops immediately evaporating. He marched forward, each step leaving wet footprints that also dried in a flash.

Elliot wondered if a sewing needle would pop the bloated water bag of a man. The ghost stopped in front of him.

"And who are you?" Elliot asked, anxious to get this visitation over with.

The ghost gurgled when he spoke, water spurting past his lips with each word. "I am the ghost of Christmas Present."

"Great. Well, let's get on with it."

The ghost nodded. He waved his hand above his head, flinging water everywhere. A fire hose shot from the back of Engine 22, swirled in the air, and then stopped with the nozzle hovering beside him. It trembled like a coiled spring ready to launch. Christmas Present hoisted his corpulent leg over the hose and straddled it. He held on to the nozzle with both hands and motioned for Elliot to climb on behind.

Elliot figured he had nothing left to lose, so he complied.

"Hold tight."

The hose jolted slightly and then shot through the front bay door. Elliot nearly fell off. He squeezed the ghost's squishy wet body as they banked right and headed down the road. It was midafternoon. The hose carried them toward downtown. Once there, they weaved in and out of holiday shoppers who carried bags and wrapped presents. Christmas Present and Elliot left the sidewalk for the busy street, dodging the many vehicles clogging downtown.

Columbus Engine 1 sat with its emergency lights flickering next to a hydrant while the crew, wearing all their fire gear, entered a high-rise building. One of them carried a water extinguisher.

"Ohhh. Should we stop and see what's happening?" Christmas Present asked.

Elliot shook his head. "Probably just a fire alarm."

Christmas Present guided the hose line to the front steps of a different skyscraper. Without slowing, they plowed through the revolving door into the lobby. Marble floors and expensive paintings on the walls told Elliot the caliber of the place. He'd never been there before. He hung on to the hose as they continued toward the closed elevator doors. They didn't stop, pouring through the doors and up the shaft toward a descending elevator car. Elliot held his breath as they blew through the car and its half-dozen passengers without even a breeze telling anyone they were there.

Elliot couldn't tell how many floors they passed, but it was a lot before they exited into another lobby. He took a few seconds to reorient himself before taking in the room. A few things immediately caught his eye. A fancy clock on the wall. A reception desk with no one sitting at it. And a dozen or so chairs on the other side of the room, only one of which was occupied.

He cocked his head. "Chloe?"

His wife sat with a manila folder clutched to her bosom. Her eyes were red and puffy and fixed on the carpet. Elliot walked to her. "Chloe? What are you doing here?"

Christmas Present answered, "She can't hear you."

Elliot huffed at him before scanning the rest of the lobby. Chloe's purse sat on the floor beside her. On a door beside the reception desk, a wooden plaque spelled out a devastating message:

McKay Family Law
We don't like divorce,
but we'll help you through it.

Elliot's knees weakened. He staggered and plopped into the chair next to her. "Chloe, has it gotten this bad? Am I that difficult to live with?"

Christmas Present asked, "Did you expect a different outcome?"

"I still love her."

"Does she know that?"

"Yeah ... I mean ... sure."

A faint vision of a different room appeared behind Christmas Past. It was blurry enough that Elliot could see the elevator through it, but it was unmistakably his kitchen. Chloe was standing by the fridge. She was crying there, too. He recognized the scene from two nights ago.

She slammed the fridge door shut. "I can't take it anymore," she snapped. "I won't."

Elliot looked to the table where his other self sat, casting a distant glare through the bay window.

"Just tell her you love her," Elliot said. But he knew he wouldn't now because he hadn't then.

Chloe stormed from the room as the vision faded away.

Elliot felt empty. "I didn't even hear her say that," he whispered.

Christmas Present shook his head, disappointed. "You don't hear much of what anyone says nowadays, do you?"

Elliot's hands dropped to his sides and he melted into the chair beside Chloe. The door with the sign opened. A slick-looking prick in a five thousand dollar pinstripe suit stood in the doorway with a phony smile. He said, "Hi, Chloe. You can come on back now."

Chloe gathered her purse and walked to him. He held the door open.

"Please stop, Chloe." Elliot reached for her back, his hand passing through her. He cried, "Don't do this. Please." The last thing he heard the lawyer say was, "Sorry your Christmas Eve has to be spent doing this crap. You'll be glad once it's finished. Trust me. Tissue?" He was such a pro he had a box at the ready. She pulled three tissues out before he set the box aside. She dabbed at her reddened nose.

The door closed. Elliot tried to follow, but bounced off the door instead. He squinted at it and reached for the handle, but his hand passed through it, just like with Chloe. He turned back, confused.

"You have seen all you are here to see," Christmas Present said. "It is time for us to leave."

Elliot was too mentally exhausted to argue. With his eyes lingering on the door, he reluctantly joined Christmas Present on the hose. They blasted through the outer wall of the office and smack into the kitchen of Station 22.

The crew sat around the two dinner tables as if a meeting had been called without Elliot being invited. One of the two lieutenants stood at the whiteboard while the other sat in one of the chairs. Greg munched on a bag of chips. Sal doodled on a magazine cover.

He enjoyed coloring in the teeth of models with a black pen. Probably something Freudian to that. Carl paced angrily between the island and the stove while Lauren rested her feet on the chair beside her. The rest of the crew filled most of the other chairs. Even Jimmy with his half-missing head sat in one of them.

Christmas Present gestured to an empty chair. "You might as well sit and listen."

The kitchen had a door with a large window that led to a small fenced-in patio. A firefighter in turnout gear who Elliot didn't recognize floated to the window. A noose hung around his overstretched neck and his head drooped awkwardly as though he couldn't lift it. He carried the charred body of a young child burned beyond recognition on his shoulders. He stopped and peered through the window, his hollow eyes weighted with the pain of the world.

Lieutenant Sanchez started the conversation. "All right. I think you all know why I called you in here." He gestured toward Lieutenant Hopkins. "We've been noticing a lot of tension here at the station lately and I have an idea why."

Carl snapped, "Elliot."

Sanchez frowned. "Let me start by saying this isn't going to be a giant bitch fest about Elliot. Is that understood?"

Most everyone nodded. Everyone except Carl.

"One bad link weakens the chain. Working with him is a nightmare, Lieu. He's an awful medic. His bedside manner is atrocious. And he's really just an all-around dick."

Sanchez lowered his head and shook it. "I guess not having a bitch fest didn't last too long, huh? I understand you're all frustrated. But we need this to be productive."

Carl wouldn't let up. "Then get him to leave the station. Have him bid out. He's ruining the crew."

Elliot lifted his middle finger. "Why don't *you* leave, Carl? Nobody's forcing you to stay."

Christmas Present held a finger to his lips. "Shhhh." He sprayed the table with water.

Jimmy sadly shook his head and then tapped his own ear.

"I am listening," Elliot snapped.

"But you're not hearing," Jimmy answered.

Greg stopped eating long enough to add, "He's right, Lieu. As much as I hate to say it, Elliot's bringing everyone down. I've tried to talk to him, but he doesn't seem to care."

Lauren raised her hand.

Sanchez nodded at her. "This is informal, Lauren. You don't need to raise your hand."

"I was just wondering, where was he earlier when our families were here? He couldn't even play nice for a minute? I know he had a rough time after Jimmy died, but Christ, that was seven years ago."

Elliot couldn't hold his tongue, regardless of whether they could hear him or not. "Yeah, seven years ago today, you assholes." He glanced at Christmas Present, annoyed.

Christmas Present stared back stoically.

Carl sat down and then stood up again. He just couldn't stand not talking. "I'm not riding with him anymore, Lieu. I'm sorry, but I can't take it. He's going to get me in trouble. Or worse, get someone killed. He's a liability."

Elliot had seen enough. He bounced up. "I get it. They don't care about me, and I don't care about them."

Jimmy bowed his head.

"What, Jimmy?" he snapped. "You just heard what they said about you. Don't you care? They act like you were never even here. They act like Katie didn't matter."

Jimmy's voice carried infinite sadness when he spoke. "They're moving on, Elliot. They're surviving the terrible things. You need to do the same."

"I can't." Elliot tried to swat a saltshaker from the table, but his hand passed through it.

Jimmy frowned. "My cruel fate is a train barreling straight for you, Elliot. You don't want what I have."

"I'm not you, Jimmy. At least your friends cared when *you* died."

The water ghost tapped Elliot's shoulder and pointed to the lieutenant who was rubbing his temples. "Listen."

Sanchez's voice was calm and gentle when he said, "I worked with Elliot as a medic years ago before I was promoted. He was a good medic. Really good. What you're seeing now isn't who he has always been. We all need to help him because he's going through something and he probably feels alone. I'm planning to have a talk with him and try to get him in to see somebody after the holidays. But I called you all in here because I need you to keep showing Elliot the same patience you have so far until he can make the turn. We don't want to lose him like we lost Jimmy."

Greg subtly nodded.

Everyone sat quietly.

Though it seemed to pain him, Carl said, "I don't want anything to happen to him, Lieu."

"I know you don't, Carl."

"It's just frustrating."

Sanchez surveyed the room. "Can you all do that for me? Can you give Elliot another chance and let me see if there's more I can do to help? If it doesn't work, I'll ask him to take a break and go to headquarters to work in the offices for a while."

Sal was one of the older firefighters, and the younger ones often looked to him for direction. He set his pen beside his magazine and lifted his chin slightly like he often did before saying something profound. Everyone watched him. Then he bobbed his head once and said, "I can do that, Lieu. Let me know what else you need."

Elliot narrowed his eyes and a confused wrinkle dented his forehead.

The rest of the crew took Sal's cue and each of them agreed. Carl was the last, but he reluctantly gave his okay as well.

A wet hand touched Elliot's shoulder. "We should go." Then Christmas Present leaned over the table and tipped the salt shaker over as if showing off.

For the first time in longer than he could remember, Elliot wanted to stay in the kitchen with the others. He wanted to hear what else they said. But he was catching on to how the visions worked. He slowly climbed back onto the hose and took one last look at his crew.

Greg went to the freezer and pulled out a popsicle. Lauren said, "Aren't you full yet, Tapeworm?"

Elliot chuckled and shook his head. The hose carried him through the station, into the parking lot, and onto Beaker Street where it stopped in front of a familiar house. Elliot recognized it even before he saw the number 375 beside the door.

"Gladys."

Christmas Present smiled and climbed from the

hose. "I think we'll walk into this one." He marched up to the salt-covered front porch and stepped aside.

Elliot followed. He leaned through the closed front door.

Inside, Gladys sat in her recliner with the light from the muted TV dancing across her robe, just as she had a few nights before. She held a picture frame against her chest. Her eyes were red, and wadded-up tissues filled a small waste can by her feet. The tissue box was empty. Her portable phone rested on the armrest and Elliot could see on the display that she had pressed 9-1-1 but hadn't hit the call button. On her tray was her blood pressure notebook with several new entries for that day.

But it wasn't the notebook or the phone or the waste can that really got Elliot's attention. Beside the notebook was a half-full glass of water and a pile of pills, many of them the same medication.

Gladys lowered the picture frame to her lap and Elliot got a look at the black-and-white photo. It was a wedding picture of her and her husband walking down the aisle. She gazed at it for a while before whispering, "Harold, I miss you so much. Why did you have to leave me?" She pulled down her glasses and wiped her eyes with a blue handkerchief. After she blew her nose, her eyes drifted to the pile of pills.

Elliot stepped forward. "Gladys?" he said. Of course, she couldn't hear him. "Don't do what you're thinking, Gladys." Elliot turned to Christmas Present, his anger burning deep. "Wake me up now. I don't want to watch this."

"Why not?" Christmas Present gurgled. "You don't give a shit anymore. Remember?"

"You're just trying to piss me off now."

The ghost grunted and opened his mouth wide,

only his voice wasn't the one that came out. It was Elliot's. "Anxiety. You've gotten yourself all worked up. You'll be fine. Just go to sleep."

Elliot's shoulders drooped. He shook his head. "That's not fair."

Christmas Present shrugged.

Gladys reached for the tray and her hand hovered over the pills. Then she reached past them to a remote control and pressed the mute button. An infomercial tried to sell her a workout machine.

Christmas Present stepped to the side to reveal two frail, emaciated children standing beside the couch. Elliot flinched. They were ghostly pale, similar in size, with wicked coal-black hair that matched the color of their dagger-like fingernails. One looked at Elliot with all the sadness of the world in his droopy eyes, while the other's face contorted in teeth-grinding rage. The sad one's face was covered in bruises and the furious one clawed at his own arm, leaving bloody trails that immediately mended back together.

Elliot tilted his head. "Oh my god. Where did you two come from? Are you all right?" He reached out to them, but the mad one snapped at his fingers with his teeth. Elliot jerked his hand back, barely avoiding losing a digit.

Christmas Present snickered. "I wouldn't get too close to them, if I were you."

Elliot glanced back to where Gladys had been sitting, but she was gone, as was her chair and her TV and her house. He was standing in an open field. "Who are these children?" he asked.

"They are my children. They are named Despair and Anger. Beware of them both. One will harm you, while the other wants to harm the world."

"Why do you show them to me?"

"Because they are inside you. They were inside Jimmy, too." He stepped in front of the children. When he moved again, they were gone. "It is time we leave."

Elliot nodded and looked for the hose line, but it was nowhere to be found. Instead, Christmas Present lunged at him with his arms extended. Elliot retreated a step before Christmas Present swallowed him into his fluid mass.

Water poured into Elliot's mouth as he tried to breathe, gagging and choking him. Panic surged to the surface as his lungs filled with water. The only thing he was more afraid of than heights was drowning.

And then he gasped and shot upright in his bed. His clock read 5:59.

"Gladys?" he whispered.

STAVE FOUR
CHRISTMAS YET TO COME

When the clock hit 6:00 AM, a low howl lifted from under Elliot's bed. A chilly upward draft made him shudder. He leaned over the edge for a peek. There was nothing but blackness below. His eyes blasted open and he retreated from the edge, holding on to the bed for dear life. He lay flat on his stomach and slowly dragged himself back for another peek. His eyes hadn't lied. His stomach turned as his bed floated over a bottomless black pit. Writhing, disfigured arms and legs and tortured faces protruded from the walls. The faces all seemed to be crying.

The invisible hand that had been dragging him around all night grabbed his upper arm and his skin sizzled under its touch. He tried to pull away, but the grip was too strong.

"What do you want me to do?" he cried.

With a violent shove, the hand flung him into the hole. Elliot screamed as he plunged through the blackness for what felt like an eternity before he saw a twinkle of light like the farthest star in the darkest of nights. The star grew and beckoned him with the promise of warmth and an end to his pain. As he fell, he involuntarily drifted to his back.

And then a strange calmness washed through him, pushing out the panic and dread. He wondered if he would fall forever—and suddenly didn't care if he did. It was magical and—

His back slammed into a medical cot with seatbelt buckles and old, dirty sheets. He scanned the inside walls of a run-down medic truck. Though he might have never been in that particular truck before, medic trucks were all basically alike, from the blue-handled trauma sheers wedged between the protective padding that lined the wall to the dollar-store plastic shower basket holding a stethoscope and the blood pressure cuff mounted with suction cups to the narrow window. It even had a ripped bench seat with orangish-yellow stuffing bulging out.

The back of the cot was raised so he could sit up. He tried to stand, but three cot straps looped over his lap, thighs, and chest, buckled, and cinched tight.

The truck bounced and rocked as if he was going somewhere fast. If not for the safety belts he'd have been tossed to the floor a dozen times over. The siren wailed outside. He looked over his shoulder toward the cab. All he saw in the driver's seat was the side of an ultra-black hood and a skeletal hand on the steering wheel. The windshield was dark as night and the wipers whipped back and forth as rain pounded the glass.

"Where are we going?" he shouted. "Let me out of here, damn it."

The ghost didn't respond.

Eventually, the medic truck stopped, its wobbly siren slowly dying like someone was strangling it. A lurching shadow swallowed him from behind and he lifted his eyes to see the cloaked figure from the driver's seat hovering silently above him. The black hood shadowed a long, narrow, pale face with a gaping mouth in the throes of a silent scream. His eyes were the blackest of pits. Elliot swallowed hard, lost in the galaxies within them. A strip of black fabric drifted past his nose. It reeked of death.

"I want to go home," Elliot whispered.

The ghost thrust his arm past Elliot's head, dragging his draping sleeve across Elliot's brow. The back doors flew open and the safety belts unbuckled. The ghost lifted the back of the cot so violently that Elliot was hurled forward and slammed face-first onto a carpeted floor. A dish-sized stain beside his head darkened the flat, worn-out maroon carpet.

He pushed himself up to look around. He was surrounded by lonely bare walls and thick curtains covering a single window. The only furnishings were a TV on a stand and a single reclining chair with its back to him. Scattered around the chair were an empty bottle of bourbon and several half-crushed Coke cans. A single boot poked out from the side.

Elliot got to his feet. A handgun lay on the floor next to the boot. Whoever was in the chair wasn't moving. "Hello?" Elliot timidly called. He scanned the room again. There was a short hallway that led to another closed door. As he looked closer at the TV, he realized a chain with a padlock was wrapped around it. A door next to the window had a "Do Not Disturb" sign hanging from the handle.

Against every urge to look away from the chair, he found his foot already taking a step toward it. "Hey," he said, and touched the top of the recliner's back. It was wet and sticky. He lifted his hand.

Blood?

Slowly, he leaned around the recliner. The first thing he saw was the dark blue of a firefighter uniform. Was this where Jimmy had ended it all? He didn't want to know. He felt a nudge at his back and turned to find the hooded ghost standing behind him.

"All right, already." Elliot searched his gut for courage and took a cautious step around the chair. He lifted his eyes to the dead man's face. His own eyes stared back with death's forever gaze. His stomach twisted and turned. He fell to his knees and vomited. "I don't want to see this anymore," he cried with his face buried in his hands.

The ghost grabbed his wrist and forced his hand away from his face. Elliot couldn't breathe. He tried to close his eyes, but some force held them open.

A small trail of dried blood stained his corpse's chin from the corner of his lips. He had seen enough exit wounds to know he didn't want to look at the back of his head.

Sudden pressure ripped through his sternum and he grabbed his chest. "Why are you showing me this?" he cried with tears streaking his cheeks. "Has this already happened? Am I a ghost like you? Am I damned like Jimmy?"

Within the hood, his guide turned his head, revealing another tortured face with its mouth sewn shut and eyes wide and blank. Then he turned his head again and a despondent face appeared. Black streaks from old tears stained his cheeks below sorrowful eyes. He offered his bony hand.

Instead of taking it, Elliot dropped forward and buried his face in the dirty carpet with his hands pressed against his ears. No one should ever see what he'd just seen. His ghostly guide stood patiently while Elliot sobbed. The pain was eternal. Once he had no more tears left, he lifted his face from the carpet and sat with his back to the wall, careful not to look at the chair again. His chest ached terribly. Approaching sirens wailed outside.

"Why haven't we left yet?" he asked. "What more can I see here?"

The ghost lowered his head and stepped aside so Elliot could see the door. Four heavy-handed thumps rattled the frame. "Fire Department," someone shouted. A ring of keys jingled. Elliot stood up and moved closer to the TV. The door swung open.

Lieutenant Sanchez rushed in first with a police officer close behind. He rounded the chair and the color instantly drained from his face. His hands went to the sides of his head and he fell to his knees. "Oh, Elliot. No."

Lauren was next in the door, and she shrieked when she saw. Sal and Greg rounded the chair. Greg's shoulders fell and Sal turned away. Carl hurried in and pressed two fingers against Elliot's carotid artery. He turned to the lieutenant, who still had a pinch of hope in his devastated face. Carl took it away with a shake of his head.

Sanchez refused to accept it. "We're working him." He yanked Elliot's body from the chair. As Elliot watched them work, the room and the crew and his body slowly faded, replaced by the same darkness that was in the ghost's eyes. His chest jolted violently with rib-cracking thumps in the rhythm of the Queen song, "Another one bites the dust." He'd used that beat for CPR many times.

He heard Carl's voice over a long, steady tone. "He's still showing a flatline, Lieu."

"We're not giving up on him. Lauren, keep doing compressions. Sal, draw me up some more epi."

Elliot opened his eyes to Lauren hovering over him, her hands thrusting against his chest. "Lauren, stop it. I'm fine."

Sanchez shoved a needle into an IV line going into

Elliot's arm. His face was racked with pain and concern. "Epi's in," he said.

Elliot tried to say something, but Lauren wouldn't stop pressing on his damn chest long enough for him to get the words out. She was going to make him sore for a week if she didn't knock it off. Carl jammed a tube into Elliot's mouth. Elliot gagged and tried to shake his head away, but Carl's ugly mug floated in front of his face. "Tube's in," he said.

Elliot shouted, "Get that fucking thing out of my mouth," but no one heard him. "Okay. Everyone settle down. Stop it. I'm fine. Go check my bunk. We're all just sleeping. This is just a dream."

The back doors of the medic truck swung open outside the emergency room entrance. As the cot pulled Elliot toward the trauma room, Elliot begged, "Will you guys cut it out. This isn't necessary. I'm fine, damn it."

Nurses and doctors swarmed him from all angles while he grew increasingly frustrated. But no matter how much he pleaded, they wouldn't stop.

Until finally they did.

The ER room fell silent. Lauren gasped and turned away. The trauma doctor shook his head. "Time of death, 10:42 PM."

Elliot sat up. He looked at his crew crying near the door. "Guys, look. I'm fine."

Sal hugged Lauren. Carl stormed through the doors, wiping his eyes. Elliot shook his head. He couldn't believe all this nonsense over nothing. A nurse dragged a white sheet over his legs. As it passed through his body toward the head of the bed, he swung his feet over the edge. He looked over his shoulder in time to see his own face staring back with death's gaze. The nurse covered it.

Everything faded to dark again. He felt the jostling of the medic truck. He opened his eyes to the yellow-orange foam poking from the ripped bench seat. A movie played across the back windows. He strained to see.

The scene drifted down from the sky to a convoy of fire engines lining the street. As the camera panned over hundreds of people standing around a blue tent, Elliot realized what he was watching. It was snowing. The crowd wore long coats and hats and gloves and stood in a sea of gravestones. The camera glided through the open flaps of the tent where a preacher stood among Elliot's closest friends and family. His entire crew was there. His mom and sister and cousins were there, too. Chloe and Riley stood crying before a casket that sat hoisted above an open grave.

Elliot had seen enough. He turned away. "I get it. It's my funeral. Fine. As if you hadn't shown me enough already." The ghost could play the movie, but Elliot didn't have to watch. He glowered at the side wall, determined not to take in even one more second of sadness.

Eventually, the medic truck slowed to a stop and his funeral stopped playing on the back windows. The doors opened to reveal the hooded ghost standing outside. He motioned Elliot toward him.

Elliot shook his head. "I'm done."

The ghost slowly shook his head and motioned him out again. Elliot sighed, slumped his shoulders, and then cautiously climbed out. The medic truck disappeared.

He stood in a long hallway with lockers lining both sides between numerous doors. A banner hanging from the ceiling read "Have A Great Christmas Break!" A janitor steered a mop bucket toward the boys' restroom. Festive streamers crisscrossed the ceiling and one of the lockers had Christmas lights adorning its door.

A bell rang and echoed through the halls. Every door swung open, almost at once. Teenagers poured from the rooms in a cacophony of unintelligible chatter.

Elliot's silent guide stood next to him. Within his hood, the ghost's head slowly turned to form a new face, strained and contorted as if wracked with pain. He lifted his finger toward one of the classrooms.

After everyone else was out of the room, one last teenager moped through the doorway. She walked alone to a locker across the hall with her head bowed. While the other kids hooted it up and laughed with their friends, she didn't talk to anyone.

Elliot's guide nudged him forward.

"Is that who I'm here to see?" Elliot asked.

The ghost gave him another push.

"All right. Fine. You can't hurt me any worse than you already have." Elliot sauntered toward the girl. Though he passed harmlessly through anyone who stepped in his way, he found himself sidestepping them as much as he could out of habit. His guide stopped him beside a small group of girls. One of them resembled his daughter's friend Stephanie, only older.

"Have you talked to her lately?" one of the other girls asked as they all watched the girl at the locker.

The one who looked like Stephanie sadly shook her head. "She's still mad at me for telling her mom about the tattoo. She won't even look at me."

"I'm worried about her. She says everything's fine, but I heard she's failing English *and* Math now."

"I know. She even quit ballet, and you know how

60

much she loves dancing. I wish she would just talk to me. I wanted to invite her and her mom over for Christmas dinner, but I know she won't come."

The group of girls went their separate ways, the one who looked like Stephanie lingering for a moment. She started to reach out toward the girl at the locker, but her hand fell back to her side. Then she hurried to her next class.

Elliot glanced over his shoulder to his waiting guide. "She seems like just another sad girl. There's a million of them. What does this have to do with me?"

His guide simply pointed again. The girl reached inside her locker. When she did, her sleeve rode up her arm enough to expose a tattoo on the inside of her forearm. Elliot strained to make it out. It was a tiny flower. A tulip.

A sick feeling crept into his gut, but he didn't immediately understand why.

She gathered her books for her next class and spun toward Elliot to leave. When she did, his eyes widened and his mouth dropped open. "Riley?" But that wasn't possible. She was only ten, and this girl was easily sixteen.

She passed through him and ice rushed through his veins. It was her. He tried to hug her, but his arms fell through nothingness. He spun to watch her walk to her next class. "What happened to her?" he shouted. "She was always so happy."

He started after her, but his guide grabbed his collar and held him back. He cried out as he watched her disappear into another classroom, trailed by a horrible sight. Christmas Present's child Despair followed her. Elliot twirled and threw his fist as hard as he could. "Let me go," he shouted. His fist passed through his guide's face and the momentum sent him sprawling to the floor. He lifted his head in the emptying hallway to see Despair's brother, Anger, glaring at him from the farthest end.

He'd thought the ghost couldn't hurt him any worse than he already had.

He was wrong.

Elliot sat up and wept.

The janitor exited the restroom and pushed his bucket down the hall. When the school bell rang again, the hallway was as empty as Elliot's heart.

A hand lifted Elliot to his feet.

"Aren't we finished yet? I don't think I can take much more."

The ghost shook his head and held up a single finger. Something pressed against Elliot's calves and forced him to sit. He was on the cot again, only this time he wasn't inside the medic truck. The straps buckled him down and the cot left the ground as his ghostly guide steered him through the ceiling. The sun was just rising and glittering off the frosted windows of the cars in a middleclass subdivision. Elliot had passed the same subdivision hundreds of times on his way home from work.

"We're going to my house, aren't we? What horrors have you got waiting for me there?"

His guide turned his head within his hood yet again. This time the ashen face was devoid of any features. No eyes. No nose or mouth. Nothing. It was blank. Flat. Empty … Dead.

His guide lowered the cot to the road about a mile from Elliot's house. Elliot climbed to his feet and regarded him. "I don't get it. You want me to walk home?"

His guide lifted a finger and pointed down the lane toward a house beyond a small patch of trees. Elliot followed his finger to a faint column of smoke lifting above the trees. He tilted his head. Something was burning, something big. He knew the family who lived there, and he knew the Andersons wouldn't be up this early in the morning. Elliot looked around for any signs that someone else had noticed the smoke and hopefully called the fire department. The street was empty.

He took a step and turned back. "I ... I should ..."

His guide nodded and flicked a hand at him.

"Yeah." Elliot started down the lane, jogging at first, and then sprinting. The smoke above the trees darkened, leaving no doubt it was the house that was on fire. He burst from the tree line and stopped dead. Smoke billowed from the Andersons' second floor windows.

The front door swung open and Mrs. Anderson stumbled onto the porch, billowing smoke chasing her. Black soot painted her cheeks and she doubled over, gagging and coughing. "Heeeelp," she screamed. "Someone, help."

Mr. Anderson stumbled out next, his arm across his eyes. Choking, he fell down the porch stairs and landed hard on the sidewalk. Mrs. Anderson shielded her face and tried to go back into the house, but heat and smoke pushed her away from the door. Frantic, she screamed, "Sarah ... Lucas." And then she fell to her knees and wailed.

Elliot stood, helpless. His head swiveled in search of someone—anyone—coming to help, but there was no one around except his guide strolling down the lane toward him. Elliot cursed him. Mrs. Anderson found her strength again and circled the house, wailing for her children as distant sirens finally broke the still morning silence.

Elliot had seen enough fatal fires to know they would be too late. His guide stopped next to him.

"I need to help them," Elliot cried.

His guide shrugged and shook his head.

"I don't understand. Why would you show me this? Are you just torturing me now? If I can't help them, why show me this?"

Standing helpless next to his silent guide, he watched as flames replaced the smoke coming from the broken windows of the second floor. Elliot wiped his eyes. The first engine company roared to the front of the house and Mrs. Anderson begged them to save her children.

The firefighters stormed the house, breathing through their masks and carrying their hose line. They didn't know it, but they were only going through the motions now. Their heroics would be for naught. They pushed themselves past the acceptable point of danger to give the children any chance of rescue, but it wouldn't be enough. Elliot didn't need to see what happened next to know the outcome.

Mr. Anderson joined his inconsolable wife next to the fire engine and held her, tears streaking his face. Elliot walked over and stood next to them. There was nothing he could do, but he hoped somehow sharing their pain would help in some spiritual way. Maybe, somehow, they wouldn't feel as alone.

More fire trucks arrived, and those firefighters desperately went to work as well. Elliot knew the feeling of giving his all despite knowing the cold reality that there was nothing left he could do.

Once the fire was out and the chief had met with all the crews, he turned and looked to the Andersons. His face said it all. He bowed his head and started toward them. The lieutenant from the first engine struggled to fight off tears.

"I've seen this scene enough times," Elliot said solemnly. "I'm ready to go."

His guide nodded. As they started walking back down the lane, Elliot heard Mrs. Anderson's ungodly scream. He looked up at his shadowy guide. "Can I go home now?"

His guide's head spun within his hood again to reveal yet another face. This one was soft and innocent and smiling. He reached out and touched Elliot's forehead with four fingers. He dragged them down Elliot's face, closing Elliot's eyes.

When Elliot opened them again, he was nestled in his bunk. His clock read 6:01. He sat up and stretched, feeling surprisingly rested.

STAVE FIVE
A NEW DAY

The bunkroom looked different that morning. Brighter, maybe. Barring an emergency call, the rest of the crew had another hour left to sleep, so Elliot crawled out of bed quietly. After he brushed his teeth and took a piss, he headed to the kitchen. When he passed the Christmas tree behind the ladder, he plugged the lights back in. He lifted his eyes to the medic truck. For the first time in years, he didn't see all the horrible things that had happened in the back. Instead, he saw a baby being delivered into his arms.

When the baby disappeared, he saw an unconscious kid turning blue because of a toy lodged in his windpipe. Elliot watched himself give the kid the luckiest squeeze possible around his abdomen just below his ribs. The toy, a mini matchbox car, shot out and nearly broke the back window. Elliot remembered it well. By the time they had reached the hospital, the kid was awake and making jokes.

Elliot looked to the cab, seeing his younger self in the passenger seat with Jimmy in the driver's seat next to him. Jimmy's face was just how Elliot remembered it, smooth and handsome. He was smiling with his strong, square jaw, undoubtedly holding back a zinger he was about to bombard the younger Elliot with. Probably something about

Elliot's receding hairline creating a fivehead instead of a forehead. Though it wasn't an original joke any of the hundred times Jimmy had launched it, he'd laughed as if it were.

As Elliot's younger self and Jimmy slowly disappeared from the front seats, a voice beside him said, "Those were the good ol' days, huh?"

Elliot nodded and turned toward the voice. Jimmy's ghost now stood beside him. Though he still glowed blue, the empty whisky bottles no longer tugged at his back. There was new strength in his posture and warmth in his smile. "How are you this morning, Elliot?" His face was whole, just like in Elliot's memory.

Elliot creased his fivehead and thought about the question for a few seconds. "I feel ... better, I think."

Jimmy nodded with an approving smile. "But your journey isn't over yet."

Elliot cocked his head. "No?"

"No. Just wanting to be better is good, but it isn't enough. You still have work to do."

Elliot listened intently.

"This is something you might not be able to do on your own. You've taken the first step, but you will need the support of your friends and family. You should take advantage of the fire department's resources and see an expert on what you're going through. Do all the things I didn't do, Elliot. Fight for it."

Elliot bobbed his head. "I will. Thank you, Jimmy."

"I'm glad I helped you start on a new path." He started to turn away, but Elliot stopped him.

"What's going to happen to *you* now?"

Jimmy looked to the sky and smiled again. "I've

made amends. You, Elliot, have helped to change my fate." His gaze lingered. Then he asked, "Will you do me one favor?"

"Anything."

"Please tell my wife and son I'm sorry for what I did … And that I love them more than anything."

"I will, Jimmy. But I think they already know."

Elliot held out his hand. When Jimmy tried to shake it, his hand passed through as he faded away.

Elliot spent the next hour making his legendary French toast, eggs, and bacon for the crew. He had it ready by the time the first of them wandered into the kitchen. It was Greg.

"Merry Christmas, Greg," he said as he fixed him a plate. Maybe the others would get a chance to eat if he controlled Tapeworm's portions up front.

Greg scrunched up his face and stared for a second. "Merry Christmas?" It was more of a question.

"Enjoy." Elliot shuffled past Greg, who still stood stunned in the doorway. He grabbed Greg's shoulder and squeezed. "Thanks for putting up with me over the last few years. I know it was tough."

"What's going on this morning, Elliot?"

Elliot paused and pondered how best to answer. "You know, Greg, sometimes being alive is all you can do. If you'll excuse me, I'm going to see if the lieutenant will let me slide out a little early today. I need to be somewhere." He hesitated a moment and then hurried back to the island and grabbed a bag of Tupperware containing two French toast breakfasts.

Lieutenant Sanchez gave him the go-ahead to cut out early. After loading the food in his truck, he scraped his windows. And then he scraped everyone else's, too.

He drove to a specific house and knocked on the

door, food bag in hand. No one answered at first and he feared the worst. Just as he was debating whether he should force open the door or not, a soft voice answered, "Coming."

Elliot sighed in relief.

Gladys opened the door. "Hello?" she said.

"Gladys, you might not remember me, but I was here a few days ago when you were having some troubles."

Her eyes brightened. "Oh, yes, honey. I remember. What are you doing here?"

"Do you like French toast?"

She nodded hesitantly.

"I know it seems strange, but I was wondering if you would be so kind as to have breakfast with me on this fine Christmas morning?"

Her eyes shrank. "I don't understand."

"No one should be alone on Christmas. I know you miss Harold."

Her hands went to her mouth. "You remembered my husband's name?"

"Of course. I bet he was a wonderful man."

"He was."

"So, what do you say? Breakfast with a dumb ol' fireman?"

The corners of her lips lifted. "I would love to. Come in."

Elliot followed her through her living room to the kitchen table. As he passed the tray beside her chair, he glanced at the pile of pills and smiled, glad that she hadn't taken them. She cleared a newspaper from the table, wet a rag, and wiped the table down. "I'm sorry for the mess, dear. I wasn't expecting company."

Elliot gave her a warm smile. "No worries."

She set out plates and forks and two glasses of

orange juice. Elliot sat across from her and asked about her husband while they ate. Her face glowed while she spoke of Harold, and Elliot spent over an hour listening to tales of her life before he caught a glimpse of the time. "Oh. Gladys, I'm sorry but I need to get home. My daughter is waiting for Santa." He got up and gathered the dishes.

"I'll get those," she said, but he wasn't having it. He filled the sink and washed them.

Gladys escorted him to the front door. As he passed her tray in the living room, he stopped. "Gladys," he said. "It looks like you've spilled your pills. May I help you clean them up?" Before she could answer, he had already gathered them into his cupped hand and was sorting them into separate piles.

"I guess I did spill them," she said as she retrieved the empty bottles from the waste bin.

After he finished, he made his way to the door. "Gladys, I want you to promise me something."

She cocked her head. "What is it?"

"I want you to promise that any time, day or night, that you feel like you need us, you will call. Will you do that?"

She tried to hide a smile as she nodded. "Then will you do one more thing for me?"

"Of course."

"Will you let me give you a hug? You've made my year this morning."

"I wouldn't leave without one."

When she hugged him, she whispered, "Thank you."

Elliot smiled and headed to his truck. He waved as he pulled away. He felt good on his drive home for the first time since he could remember. After he pulled into his driveway, he sat in his truck watching his front door for a few minutes before he found the strength to get out. He wished he had a gift for his wife, but time had beaten him to the store.

He opened his front door. Chloe happened to be walking past as she went to the Christmas tree in the formal living room. She had always done a great job of decorating for the holidays and the house looked spectacular. He was surprised he hadn't noticed over the past few weeks. Under the tree sat a dozen or more gifts, wrapped and waiting for Riley's big moment.

Chloe barely said hi.

"Mom," Riley shouted from upstairs. "Is that Dad? Can I come down now?"

Elliot looked to the top of the stairs. "It's me, Tulip. Come on down."

She could've given the roadrunner a race with how fast she cleared the stairs. "Hi, Dad," she blurted as she zipped past him to the tree. She dug into the first present, an odd-shaped gift with a bow.

Elliot reached for Chloe's hand. She looked down, surprised. He pulled her to him. Despite Christmas being her favorite time of year, her eyes were heavy. She gazed at his chest as though she couldn't look at his face.

Riley set an ice castle playset aside and dove for another present, discarded wrapping paper quickly piling around her. Elliot touched Chloe's chin and gently lifted it. Their eyes met. He filled his with sincerity. "I want to fix us, Chloe. I want to fix me. If it's not too late."

Tears blurred her eyes.

He almost couldn't speak. "I'm so sorry for everything. I'll do whatever it takes to make things right. I may need help, but I'll do it. I just need you to be with me while we get through this together."

"Socks," Riley shouted. "I love them."

Chloe held his gaze for a few seconds. The wait for her answer was torture. Then she nodded, and that simple action released a year's worth of tears. As she sobbed, he pulled her cheek to his chest. She squeezed him as hard as she could.

He wiped his own eyes. "Thank you for sticking with me through all of this so far. I know it was hard."

Riley tugged Chloe's robe. "Mom, why are you crying?" she asked. She offered a small gift that she had obviously wrapped on her own. "Here. This will make you happy."

Chloe took the present and laugh-cried. "I am happy, honey."

Elliot put his arm around Chloe's shoulders and together they walked to the couch. It might have been the best Christmas ever. After the presents were opened and they had finished breakfast, Elliot excused himself to sneak up to the bedroom. With no one around, he retrieved his handgun from the bedside table and locked it in his gun safe, determined to never get it out again.

EPILOGUE

Three years passed. Elliot's marriage was going strong with the help of counseling and a lot of understanding. The fire department's Employee Assistance Program had been a godsend. Riley was thriving in school and getting all A's, and had joined a well-known ballet studio. Elliot didn't care what anyone else said; he was convinced she was the best dancer in the studio. Well, she hadn't gotten into any productions yet, but that didn't dampen his pride. At every opportunity, he initiated heart-to-hearts with her about how she was doing, sometimes to her very boisterous annoyance.

Life wasn't perfect, though. Periods of sadness still broke through and he needed to be careful. He was fortunate to have learned how to better recognize his triggers early and seek whatever help he needed before the sadness dug in too deep. It was an ongoing struggle, but one he felt he was winning.

Elliot's phone alarm woke him early Christmas morning. It was his last Christmas at Station 22. He was being promoted to lieutenant starting on the next duty day and would spend the next few years filling in at one of the other thirty-plus stations. He couldn't wait to have enough seniority to get a permanent assignment.

The crew had given him a nice send-off the night before. There was even a cake that read in green icing:

~~Better luck next time!~~
We knew you could do it!

Lieutenant Sanchez had presented him with a wheeled bag to carry his turnout gear from station to station. "An essential," he'd said, "for when you live out of your truck over the next few years."

Elliot quietly made French toast, eggs, and bacon for the crew and then slipped out early for his annual breakfast with Gladys. She still said it was the bright spot of her year, which made him as sad as it did happy.

As he drove home, he imagined how Riley was going to react to her new iPhone from Santa. He couldn't wait to see her face. His truck followed the road as if it knew the way while he daydreamed and took in the sights. He'd made the final turn toward his house when he caught something out of the corner of his eye.

Smoke above the Andersons' house.

His stomach dropped. He dialed 9-1-1 and gunned his truck toward the house. The dispatcher answered and he reported a fire "with people trapped" as he sped along the narrow lane through the patch of trees. The smoke was darkening. Elliot slid to a stop in the driveway and bounced from the cab.

Mrs. Anderson stumbled from the front door and fell to her knees. Elliot ran to her. "Where are the kids?" he shouted.

She was coughing too much to speak, but she pointed toward the upstairs. Elliot stormed the front door as Mr. Anderson tumbled out. Elliot dropped to his knees and held his breath. He crawled inside, but the smoke was too thick and hot and it pushed him back to the porch.

He scanned the house for another way in, but he knew the back door would be just as bad. Distant sirens announced help was on its way, but they were still too far away.

Elliot raced to his truck and jumped behind the wheel. He gunned the engine and slammed into the side of the house beneath a bedroom window. After digging through his spare tire kit for a tire iron, he climbed onto the roof of his truck.

He closed his eyes and bashed out the window above his head. Pieces of glass dug into his palms as he pulled himself inside. The smoke tasted like razorblades. His eyes immediately watered and burned, so he shut them. There was so much smoke he couldn't see anyway.

He shoved his head out the window for one last deep breath and then crawled into the bedroom.

He shouted, "Lucas. Sarah." Someone coughed and gagged within the smoke-filled darkness. Elliot scrambled toward the sound, sweeping his hand along the floor like he'd been taught. His fingers brushed something soft. He grabbed a leg.

Jackpot.

Using the wall to find his way back to the window, he carried the child to the sill. It was Sarah. She was only ten. Elliot took her hands as his brain threatened to pop without fresh air. He leaned out the window and lowered her to the roof of his truck. With his head below the sill and the smoke pouring out above him, he breathed in fresh air. Then he ducked back inside.

He found Sarah's bedroom door partially open. The fire crackled downstairs and the intense heat threatened to melt his skin. He didn't waver despite the pain. Staying as low as he could, he made his way to the next open door. Punishing blisters lifted on the back of his neck and the side of his face seared.

He scrambled into the next bedroom and closed the door to buy himself a small reprieve from the heat. "Lucas," he screamed. No one answered. He strafed the room on his hands and knees until he found a body next to the closet. He pulled the boy close to his chest and felt for his heartbeat. The kid had a chance.

He carried Lucas to the bedroom window and shoved it open. There was no time to wait for a ladder from the fire department, so he grabbed Lucas's hands and lowered him through the window. Then he climbed onto the sill and wedged his feet against the corners of the frame.

He lowered Lucas close enough to the ground that when his feet slipped from the window, the boy wasn't injured in the fall. Elliot tucked his head and landed hard on his left shoulder and arm. A bone in his upper arm snapped. As he rolled to his back and lay next to the unconscious boy, he heard the firefighters hurrying around the house. He couldn't see through his watery eyes, but he heard them grab Lucas and rush off.

Another firefighter knelt beside him and said, "We're gonna get you help, buddy. You've got some pretty bad burns."

Elliot coughed and gagged and rolled back to his side. He felt the world fading. He remembered Jimmy and the ghosts and the lessons they had taught him. He felt weightless as the firefighters lifted him and carried him away.

He wasn't ready to die.

He was ready to sleep, though.

Elliot didn't feel any pain.

Someone whispered his name. It sounded like Chloe.

His eyes fluttered and he strained to open them against the brightness overhead. A blurry silhouette stood over him. His throat was raw like he had swallowed bleach.

"Elliot?" Chloe said again.

He tried to answer, but he couldn't talk. He blinked away the haze as his eyes adjusted to the brightness. Chloe leaned over him, a smile painted across her face. "Don't try to talk, honey. There's a tube down your throat."

She turned toward the door and called for a nurse. Then she grabbed a newspaper from a table. She held the front page so he could see. The headline read: "Hero Off-duty Firefighter Saves Two Children."

"That's about you, baby. You saved the Anderson kids."

He tried to ask if they were okay, but he couldn't make any sounds. She retrieved the bed controls and lifted his head. She pointed to the bathroom door, which was covered with probably a hundred get-well cards. "Those are just from strangers. I have another whole stack that there wasn't room for."

Lt. Sanchez accompanied a nurse through the door. His smile filled the room. "Elliot, you son of a gun. You had us worried. The crew has been taking shifts to be here when you woke up. Looks like I won."

Chloe interjected, "Don't let him fool you. He's been here almost the entire time. Since I don't think the man sleeps, it would have been hard for him to not be here when you woke up."

Sanchez shrugged. As he described nearly the entire fifteen-hundred-member-strong fire department showing up at one point or another while Elliot was unconscious, Riley appeared in the doorway behind him. She had happy tears on her cheeks.

Elliot lifted his good arm toward her. It hurt like hell to move his other arm, so he left it at his side. It was in a cast. Gauze covered part of his face and he was afraid to let Riley see. She stormed in and nearly smothered him in a hug. Despite the rapidly growing need for the morphine that the nurse was drawing up, Elliot couldn't be happier. He thought about Jimmy and the other ghosts and couldn't imagine what would have happened without them. He was glad he lived. He was glad he could help the Andersons. And he was glad he was a firefighter.

END

If you need help, get help now. Do it today or tonight or whenever you're reading this. As long as you're still here, there's time. We want you in this world. I want you in this world.

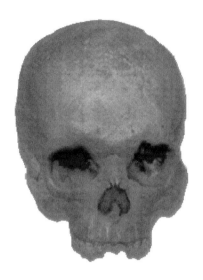

JANITOR

"If you are physically sick, you can elicit the interest of a battery of physicians; but if you are mentally sick, you are lucky if the janitor comes around." ~Martin H. Fischer

NIGHT ONE

Bill met Jeb outside the factory as usual. "I lost my keys, Jeb. You'll have to crawl in through the window again."

Jeb nodded at the friendly security guard. "You gotta stop losing those. I hate crawling through the window." He stared at his hands.

Bill hesitated. "You all right today, buddy?"

"Um-hm. Just tired." Jeb shoved the piece of wood covering the window aside and started climbing through. He was happy to get inside where it was warm. The Christmas season in Ohio could get pretty chilly.

"Jeb?" Bill called out.

Jeb froze with a leg still out.

"You ain't been acting yourself lately. You sure you're all right?"

"I'm sure. Christmas is just a little tough since my ma died."

"I know you two were close. I'm sorry."

"I never lived by myself until then. I don't much like it."

"Yeah, I don't suppose you do. It's been a few years, though. It's not getting any better?"

"Not really."

Jeb climbed the rest of the way inside. He'd always liked Bill, or Duck Bill as he called him under his breath. Jeb had secret nicknames for everyone he met. Like the girl at Starbucks, Mocha Mama. Or the police officers who'd waved at him as he drove to work three days ago—he called them the Blue Man Group.

With Duck Bill gone, Jeb secured the window board with a stick and started yet another long, lonely night in the cold, dank factory. His iPod was his only companion. Though it would hold up to twenty thousand songs, he was content with a single hour's worth. After all, why have thousands of songs when the sixteen he had were the best?

He looked at his watch. 11:07. Perfect. Right on time. He pressed play.

The first song always got his blood pumping. Johnny Cash couldn't be beat. As Mr. Cash's unique pipes sang about the man in black, Jeb sang along without missing a word.

Jeb made his way to the utility closet and filled a mop bucket. After dunking his mop, he squeezed the bucket handle tight against it three times—always three times—to drain the sudsy water. He swooshed his mop over the rough entranceway linoleum. There was one particular yellow stain on the white floor that he spent an extra moment scrubbing with the plastic part of the mop. Though he knew it wouldn't come clean that day any more than it had any other day over the last six months, he always gave it a little extra love.

Johnny continued singing while Jeb dragged his yellow mop bucket through the double doors and into the bathroom. One of the bucket's wheels stuck and splashed the filthy water on his pant leg, but he didn't care. He'd wash his pants three times when he got home whether they were dirty or not.

He knocked on the ladies' room door. No one answered, of course, but he cracked the door and said,

"Hello?" just to be safe.

Mick Jagger screamed about Angie in his ears, which told him he was right on schedule. He finished the linoleum office floors at 1:29 AM and then scuttled to the breakroom and the snack machine for his 1:30 oatmeal cream pie.

He slipped his fifty-five cents into the machine and groaned in delight with his first delicious bite. He was two-thirds through his snack when a loud clatter echoed from the hall. He nearly choked on his snack. "Hello?" he called. He tugged one of his earpieces from his ear.

No one answered. He stood motionless with the rest of his oatmeal cream pie dangling at his side. He didn't move again through all of "Beth" by KISS and partway into "Sweet Home Alabama."

After a mental pep talk, he decided to take a look. He set his cream pie on the edge of the table and tiptoed to the door.

"Is someone there?" he whispered, praying no one would answer. He turned the handle as quietly as he could. The door seemed to weigh a ton.

After a deep breath, he leaped into the hallway and landed in some kind of made-up kung fu stance. He wasn't sure what he would do if someone was actually there, but he knew he would do something. Most likely scream and run.

His mop handle had fallen across a table and a coffee mug lay shattered on the floor. *Mental note: Secure the handle against the wall from now on.*

A low buzz from above grabbed his attention. He slowly lifted his eyes to a fluorescent light flickering as if possessed. His shoulders slumped. *Damn it.* Between changing the bulb and cleaning up the mug, his schedule was screwed.

He picked up the big pieces and carried them to the trashcan inside the break room. Then he dug out the dustpan and tiny broom from under the sink. When he went back into the hall, there was another mug shattered under the table. He stopped and scratched his head. How in the hell had he missed the second mug before? He didn't have time to ponder. First the mugs, then the light. The Statler Brothers sang about flowers on their walls to remind him of how far behind he was, and he still had to change the bulb. He might need to skip lunch. He worked slowly and methodically.

Skipping lunch was the right call. He managed to finish his routine just before the morning crew arrived. He stuck his dying iPod and rolled-up earbuds into his pocket. Since Bill was the only one with the keys (when he didn't lose them), Jeb had to climb out the window. The first worker pulled into the lot as Jeb was pulling out.

NIGHT TWO

"Good night, Jeb," Duck Bill called out when Jeb showed up for his next shift.

Before Bill could cross the parking lot, Jeb hurried to catch him. "Hey, Bill. Can I ask you something?"

Bill shrugged. "Sure."

"Have you ever seen anyone in here at night who shouldn't be?"

"Not a chance. Why?"

"Oh, I don't know. Just wondering, is all." Jeb picked at one of his fingernails as Bill started to leave again.

"Hey, Bill," Jeb blurted, stopping his friend once more. "Guess what?" Without waiting for an answer, he said, "I met a girl."

"Yeah? That's great. What's her name?"

Jeb's eyes nervously wandered. His face grew flushed.

"Well, Jeb?" Duck Bill's mouth slanted and he grinned. "What's her name?"

"Becky," Jeb mumbled with his head bowed, too embarrassed to look at his friend. "She works at Starbucks."

"Well, good for you, Jeb. Good for you." Duck Bill patted Jeb's shoulder. "I'll see you tomorrow, bud." He whistled as he crossed the parking lot. He must have lived somewhere close because he never drove a car. Jeb climbed through the window and got to work. He shoved the earbuds into his ears and pressed play.

He was already two minutes behind. Thoughts of blue-eyed Becky filled his mind as he sang along with his music.

By 3:00 AM Jeb realized that, for the first time since he had started working at the factory, his music fell on preoccupied ears. His entire night had been spent thinking about Becky and her perfectly straight blond hair.

Until his dying day, he wouldn't forget her number—not just because it was hers, but because the last four digits spelled JOHN. Just like Johnny Cash.

He scrubbed a greasy handprint from high up on a second-floor window and cursed the factory workers for what he was sure was a prank. After all, how could a handprint get up there if it wasn't some kind of joke? The window cleaning took him even more out of his routine than the light bulb had because he was a bit of a perfectionist and decided to wash all the windows so they'd match.

His doctor had told him that changing up his routine was healthy and recommended it whole-heartedly. Maybe Doctor Denoble was the one who put the dirty print on the window as a test. But that didn't make sense. When would his doctor have time to visit the factory? Besides, Jeb didn't remember telling him where he worked. He should probably keep that theory to himself. If he asked Doctor Denoble about it, the doctor would probably increase his meds. And Jeb could just imagine how pissed he'd be when he learned Jeb hadn't been taking them.

The factory had more pain-in-the-ass windows than a solarium, and washing them took nearly two cycles of his playlist. He finished at the very window where he had begun, put his window cleaner back into his cart, and admired the shining results of his work.

Until he saw it.

What the f—? The first window now sported another handprint near its top, identical to the print that started his whole window-washing adventure … only the new print appeared to be on the outside.

He scanned the factory and the parking lot for any possible culprits. His pulse throbbed in his throat. He was too far off schedule already. Besides, outside window washing was a summer job. Still, it nearly killed him to ignore the new handprint and get back on schedule.

He'd started pushing his cart to the next area he was going to clean when a loud clang suddenly sent the factory into darkness. Luckily, a full moon gave enough light through the windows that he could still see to get to the breakroom where there was a flashlight. He hated when the lights went out, which seemed to happen once a week at least. Going to the basement to reset the breaker box was the worst part of his job. The basement gave him the creeps.

He found the flashlight in the cupboard and made his way to the basement door. There was no use in hurrying now. His schedule was shot. He'd be lucky to get the trash emptied before the morning shift arrived.

Each step down the basement stairs was more terrifying than the one before. Something scurried across the floor and Jeb shot the flashlight beam toward two small, glowing eyes in the corner. His heart stuttered. He prayed it was a rat and not a raccoon. He hated raccoons, especially after startling one that had been eating in the dumpster at his apartment complex when he was younger. He had gotten nearly a hundred stitches as his reward.

The two eyes scrambled into a small hole in a

waterlogged box that sagged to one side. He stepped off the stairs into an inch or so of water. He was glad he wasn't the one who dealt with water leaks because this was a mess. If he remembered, he'd leave the boss a note.

He slogged through the standing water to the breaker box and opened the door. He worried about flipping a breaker while standing in water, but he didn't have much choice. He timidly reached into the box and touched the breaker. Wincing and holding his breath, he flipped it down.

The furnace behind the stairs kicked on with a grunt and a groan. Jeb closed the breaker box and turned back to the stairs. His heart jumped. A beast of a man stood on the stairs. Jeb yelped. His back met the breaker box. "Wh-wh-who are you?" he asked.

The man didn't answer. The brim of a dark hat shadowed his pale, square face. An unlit cigarette hung from his bluish lips.

"What are you doing in here?" Jeb asked. He tried to sound strong, but his voice wobbled.

The big man's cigarette dropped to the step and he crushed it with his foot. Then he stepped down.

"Don't come near me," Jeb cried.

Once the man reached the last step, he lunged and grabbed Jeb's shirt, ripping two buttons from his collar.

"What did I do?" Jeb cried.

The man heaved him hard against the stairs. Jeb's back struck the edge of one of the steps and the air vomited from his lungs. His precious iPod slid across the concrete step, ripping the buds from his ears. The man grabbed a rusty wrench from the sagging box and heaved it at Jeb's head. Blood exploded from Jeb's nose as the wrench bounced off his face and then splashed onto the flooded floor.

Frantic, Jeb scrambled up the stairs, his eyes locked on his large attacker who stood motionless at the bottom. Jeb slammed the basement door shut and slid a wheeled press machine in front of it. He flipped the brake down with his foot and leaned against the machine to catch his breath. He pinched his bleeding nose. He'd never been in a fight before, not even when the other kids had bullied him in school, and his hands trembled. Every hair stood up on his arms.

After a quick scan of the factory floor, he sprinted to the breakroom and pushed a table against the door. Grabbing the coffee pot to use as a weapon, he turned to the phone hanging on the wall. The "Out of service" sign was a kick in the gut. With his eyes trained on the only way in or out of the breakroom, he sat in one of the chairs and pressed a napkin against his throbbing nose. It took at least ten minutes before the bleeding slowed and his heart stopped racing.

He sat alone for the rest of the night, his eyes never leaving the door. When the sun peeked through the breakroom window and it was time to leave, he found some courage he didn't know he had and cautiously crept into the hall. To get out, he needed to pass the basement door, a terrifying prospect. With his head on a swivel, he carefully approached. The wheeled press machine sat crooked in front of the half-open basement door. That was all Jeb needed to see. He ran to the broken window and climbed through. Maybe he should have waited around and told the morning crew about the man dressed all in black, but they had Boxing Phil on their crew and Boxing Phil could take on anyone.

Jeb was gone before the morning shift arrived.

NIGHT THREE

Jeb struggled all day with whether to go back to work or not, but in the end he couldn't leave his boss hanging. Before he left his apartment he found his granddad's old pocketknife and shoved it in his pocket.

Duck Bill met him in the back by the parking lot like always. When Jeb approached, Bill tilted his head and squinted. "What happened to your face?" he asked. Duck Bill and Best-girl Becky were the only two people who would even notice or care that he had a swollen nose and a black eye.

"I bumped it last night on the press machine," he answered, using the same story for Bill as he had for Becky when she'd asked why he sounded so nasal on the phone earlier.

"Ouch. It looks sore."

"You don't even know."

Jeb was dying to tell Bill about the big man in black, but he didn't want one of his only friends to think he was as crazy as everyone else did. He'd been told that plenty of times in his life.

"Hey, Jeb. I still haven't found my keys. You're gonna have to climb through the window again. Just make sure to secure it once you're inside."

Jeb was getting tired of crawling through the window just to go to work. They should have given him his own keys when he started. "You need to find those keys, Bill. What are you going to do when they finally fix the window?"

"Oh, I'll find them by then."

Bill started to turn away, but turned back. He held out Jeb's black iPod and white earbuds. "Oh yeah. I found this in the breakroom. It's not like you to leave your music behind."

In the breakroom? Jeb snatched the iPod and thanked his friend. He climbed through the window and jammed the stick against the frame to secure it. He double-checked that the stick was firmly in place. And then triple-checked. He debated whether to listen to music or not, and decided if he left one earbud out he would hear if anyone got in again. He couldn't live without his Johnny Cash.

He pressed play.

Jeb swept and mopped and cleaned the toilets, never allowing himself to be completely immersed in his songs or his thoughts. Billy Joel singing about being the piano man for the fifth time of the night meant it was time to take out the trash. And he dreaded taking out the trash.

He didn't need keys to go out the back door as long as he didn't let it slam shut. He made seven trips with seven bags to the back door and stacked them, part of him hoping some magical genie would show up and carry them out. But, alas, there were no genies. He wiped his feet three times on the doormat before slinging the door open. For this part of the job, he shoved his earbuds into his pocket, though he left the iPod playing so as to not screw up his routine.

In the alley, a motion-sensing security light blinked to life, its cone highlighting the dumpster and little else. Jeb's eyes danced side to side.

He hated to go out, but at least he wasn't going out completely helpless. Not with his granddad's pocketknife. He brushed his hand over his pocket just to make sure it was still in there. Then he stepped away from the safety of the doorway.

With his eyes peeled, he quickly carried bag after bag to the dumpster and tossed them into the green behemoth. Once the last bag was gone, he slammed the metal lid closed and spun back toward the door. His every muscle flinched. He nearly lost control of his bladder. *Oh no.*

The bastard from the night before filled the doorway. He wore a long black coat with broad shoulders. Seeing him again, Jeb wasn't so sure Boxing Phil *could* handle him. Quiet and calm, the giant glared across the alley. His eyes could wilt steel. He wasn't wearing a hat this time and his jet-black hair was slicked back like a character from *The Sopranos*. He held an unlit cigarette between his lips. For one insane second, Jeb wondered if the stranger was death himself.

"Who are you?" Jeb asked, his voice a quivering mess.

The man didn't answer.

Jeb's eyes drifted to the open end of the alley and the man moved to cut off his escape.

"What do you want?" Jeb shouted.

Still the man didn't answer. He stepped toward Jeb, and Jeb stepped back toward the dumpster.

"Why?" Jeb cried.

The man silently advanced. Jeb threw his arms in front of his face and cowered against the dumpster. The man stopped only a few feet away. The air thickened between them. The man's upper lip curled and his cigarette fell from his mouth. Jeb couldn't hear anything but his own heartbeat.

"We can work this out. Whatever you want, I'll get

for you."

The man pounced. He was faster than his size suggested. Jeb closed his eyes. The man grabbed his wrist with such strength that Jeb's forearm nearly snapped.

Jeb dug into his pocket with his free hand and pulled out his granddad's beat-up pocketknife. It was so old and lose he could sling it open with one hand. He blindly stabbed at the man's arm. Just before pay dirt, the man released his wrist and Jeb's blade sank into his own flesh. He grabbed his forearm and collapsed to his rear. He squeezed, helpless to mute the stinging pain.

The big man towered over him, his eyes coal-black and distant with nothing behind them.

"Why are you doing this to me?" Jeb screamed. "I thought we had a deal."

The man shook his head.

THE MAN IN BLACK

The handle of Jeb's knife protruded from his own forearm as he scooted along the front of the dumpster and away from the big man in black. The man stood quietly and watched.

Jeb braced himself against the dumpster to stand up. "It's not fair," he cried. "I did the classes like I was supposed to. I just don't like the meds. They make me feel weird."

The man stood stoic.

"It's not going to happen again," Jeb screamed. He slowly circled the man, heading toward the open end of the alley. Surprisingly, this time the man didn't block his path. As Jeb backed away, he clenched his teeth and pulled his pocketknife from his arm. It hurt as bad coming out as it had going in. He folded it closed and stuffed it back into his pocket. With his palm shoved against the bleeding wound, he sprinted for the parking lot. He didn't look back, fearing the big man would be on his heels. His arm throbbed and spurted blood between his fingers with each frantic beat of his heart.

His silver Ford Taurus was the only car in the lot. As he ran to it, he dug through his pocket for his keys before slamming into the car door. "Come on, come on," he whispered, fumbling through his many keys for the right one. Once he found it, he jammed it into the lock.

Too terrified to look back, he climbed into the

driver's seat and shoved the key into the ignition with one hand steadying the other.

The engine sputtered to life. He slammed the gear shift into drive and mashed the gas pedal. As he sped through the parking lot toward the only exit, the big man appeared in his path beneath the only working streetlight in the lot. He held something at his side. Jeb slammed on the brakes.

They glared at each other for what felt like a lifetime.

Then the man lifted his hand. Jeb's headlights beamed on a green apron clutched in his fist.

It was a Starbuck's apron. *No, no, no. Becky.* "What did you do to Becky, you bastard?" Fire surged through his veins. He lifted his foot from the brake pedal and stomped on the gas. The big man stood firm. Jeb closed his eyes. He felt the impact through the steering wheel and opened them in time to see the man in black tumble over the hood, smash the windshield, and roll over the roof. Jeb leaned around the smashed part of the windshield an instant before he crashed into the streetlight. The airbag blasted his face. He flopped back into the seat. Airbag dust choked him and burned his eyes. Steam sprayed from beneath his crumpled hood.

He rubbed his irritated eyes. He turned the key, but his car gurgled, as dead as he was about to be. His eyes shot to the rearview mirror where a body should have been. Nothing. A look out both side windows revealed no one there either. He tugged the handle and flung the door open. As he stumbled out of the car, he scanned the empty lot again for the big man's body, knowing he had hit him pretty hard.

Something wet and warm trickled down his forehead and he gingerly touched it. Blood. But he didn't have time to worry about his own injuries. He needed to call Becky. He stumbled toward the exit. He whispered, "Where are you going?"

Then he answered himself, "To find a phone."

"No. Not this time."

He pressed his palms hard against his head and squeezed his eyes closed. *It can't be happening again.*

He needed to call Becky. She would get him straight. He took off in a sprint toward his apartment two miles away. But two miles for someone who hadn't run in a long time and maybe never that far was tougher than he expected. A sudden stitch in his side nearly threw him to the pavement, but he pushed through it.

He'd never been so happy to see his apartment building.

Gasping for air, he barreled into the door to the lobby and then ripped it open. After pressing the elevator "up" button three times, he decided to take the stairs. He skipped every other step on his way to the third floor. Once through his apartment door, he secured it with a deadbolt. Then he unlocked the deadbolt, locked it, unlocked it again, and locked it a third time. His studio shack seemed smaller and darker than ever before.

"What do I do?" he whispered.

"Wait for him to come," he answered. "He'll help you."

"Shut up." He grabbed his telephone and dialed Becky's number, mumbling, "J-O-H-N," as he dialed the last four digits. *Pickuppickuppickup.*

Instead of Becky's voice, he heard a tone followed by the operator's recorded message for a nonworking number.

"Damn it." He must have dialed wrong. He tried again. After another recording, he slammed the portable phone on the counter.

He ran to the kitchen cupboard where he kept all his meds. The first pill bottle he pulled out was empty. So was the second. He stuck his hand into the cupboard and emptied it with a wide, sweeping motion. Empty bottles spilled to the floor.

"It's not fair," he cried. A faint memory surfaced of him standing over the toilet, dumping pills in the bowl and flushing them down. He plopped to his rear and pulled his knees to his chest with his back against the counter. *I thought I was better.*

Just when he couldn't take the silence any longer, there was a knock on his door. Jeb slowly lifted his head. "Leave me alone," he shouted.

The voice that returned was like a song. "Jeb?" Becky asked. "What's wrong?"

Jeb raced to the door, fumbled with the lock, and then ripped it open. He grabbed Becky's hand and yanked her into the apartment, slamming the door shut behind her. After locking and unlocking the deadbolt three times, he spun around. "You shouldn't have come here, Becky."

"Why? What do you mean? You called me and told me to come over. You said you had an emergency."

"No, I didn't. I mean, it wasn't me." Jeb grabbed Becky's shoulders and locked eyes with her. "You're in danger. You have to leave."

"I don't understand." She looked at the dried blood on his forehead and gently touched his wound. "Oh my god. What happened?"

"It's nothing. He's coming for us. Do you have anyone who can help us?"

"I … I …"

"Forget it. I know who can help. I'll call Duck Bill. He'll know what to do." Jeb pounded his fists against his temples. *Think, damn it. What's Bill's number?* He realized Bill had never given it to him. Maybe the factory had it. Someone should be there by now. He grabbed his phone and dialed.

A woman's voice answered. "Tectrum Industries. This is Suzie. How may I help you?"

"Suzie, it's Jeb. I need Bill's number right away."

"Jeb?"

"Yeah, you know, the night janitor. I need the security guard Bill's phone number. It's an emergency."

"Uhhh." She paused. "I don't know anyone working here named Bill. Or Jeb, for that matter. We don't have a night janitor. Are you the one who's been breaking in here at night?"

He must have dialed another wrong number. He hung up and dialed again.

"Tectrum Industries. This is Suzie. How may—"

Jeb threw the phone against the wall. Were they pissing with him?

He turned to Becky and she cowered away from his outstretched hand. "What's wrong? I won't hurt you."

She nodded past his shoulder. Jeb spun back to the wall where he had smashed the phone.

The man in black stood beside the sliding door to his balcony. Jeb's eyes narrowed. It was impossible. He was sure he had locked the sliding doors. It was part of his routine. Even if the door was unlocked, the giant of a man couldn't have climbed the three stories to his balcony. "How did you get in here?" he shouted.

The big man didn't answer.

Jeb nudged Becky behind him and puffed out his

chest like a comic book superhero. "Get in the bathroom," he said. He pushed her toward the bathroom door. When she was safely inside, he closed the door. He'd always wanted to be a hero, and having Becky there gave him the courage.

"Jeb," she shouted through the door. "You need to come in here. I need you to see something."

He ignored her and grabbed the only weapon close by—a set of pliers from his table. He had forgotten about his granddad's pocketknife. Drawing from every action movie he'd ever seen, he said, "Just you and me, big man," and lunged.

Effortlessly, the man grabbed his arms and yanked the pliers from his hand. He spun Jeb around and bear-hugged his squirming body from behind.

"What do you want?" Jeb pleaded.

The hulk grabbed Jeb's hair and held him still. Jeb kicked and thrashed to no avail. The big man pinched Jeb's cheek hard with the pliers. Jeb grunted and grabbed his attacker's thick hands, desperately trying to stop him. The bastard squeezed, twisted, and yanked. The flesh and muscle ripped and popped from Jeb's cheek. Jeb cried out with a deafening shriek.

The big man dropped Jeb to his knees and backed up. Jeb turned wet, terrified eyes on him. "Why did you do this to me?"

For the first time, the man spoke. With a nod to Jeb's hands, he said, "Look, Jeb."

Jeb reluctantly lowered his eyes to his own blood-covered hands. The pliers, along with the butchered meat from his face, rested in his own open palm.

He looked back up at the man. "I don't understand."

The man stood emotionless.

Jeb dropped the pliers and stood up. When the man didn't attack, he raced to the bathroom door. "Let me in, Becky," he whispered. He turned the handle and the door opened.

Becky wrapped her arms around him as he closed the door. For the first time in his life he felt wanted. He was her hero. Though his face throbbed, he found a smile. "I love you, Becky."

She slowly pulled away and whispered, "I know you do. But there's something you should know."

"What is it?"

"Look in the mirror." She guided his chin toward his reflection.

"I know. That bastard hurt my face. But I'll get him for you. I'll protect you."

"No. Not that."

Jeb frowned. "What, then?"

"Just look. It's happening again. You need help."

He sluggishly turned his head.

His reflection stared back at him, but there was something wrong. Yes, he had a gaping hole in his face, his chin was covered in blood, and his nose was swollen and bruised, but that wasn't what she was trying to tell him. He stood staring into the mirror with Becky at his side. Only Becky's reflection wasn't there.

No, please. Don't let it be true. Not this time.

He turned back to Becky, but she was gone. *Oh no. Not again.*

Someone pounded on his front door. He ripped the bathroom door open. The big man still stood in the front room. The pounding came again. "Police," a man's voice shouted.

Jeb wasn't going to fall for that again. The man in black looked at the door and whispered, "They probably found your car. You'd better let them in."

Jeb ignored him. "What are you doing to me?" he screamed.

With a sad smile, the big man answered. "I'm not doing this, Jeb. You're doing it to yourself. You need help again. Let the authorities help you."

"No." Jeb had been so sure he was cured. Doctor Denoble had said he was doing so well.

"Open the door, sir," the officer outside shouted.

"Leave me alone," he shouted back.

The man in black sauntered to the sliding door and opened it. He looked over his shoulder. "Let them help you, Jeb."

Jeb thought about Becky and wondered what the bastard had done with her. "I'll kill you," he screamed and charged.

The police officer shouted, "Open the door now or I'm coming in."

Jeb slammed into the man in black with such force he sent him tumbling over the edge. Sirens echoed from the street. The front door crashed open.

Jeb spun toward it. Somehow, the man in black was now in the doorway. He said, "Easy, mister. I'm here to help."

Jeb remembered his granddad's pocketknife and crammed his hand into his pocket.

"Sir, get your hands out of your pockets," the man in black shouted. He lifted a gun. He was wearing a badge.

Jeb's fingers brushed the pocketknife. He pulled it out and unfolded it.

"Sir, put the knife down," the man in black shouted.

Jeb shook his head. "You're not going to do this to me again," he screamed as he took an aggressive step forward.

"Please, sir. Put down the knife. Don't make me shoot you. Please."

Jeb scoffed. It was a bluff. The man in black would never shoot him. He never had before. "I know what you did with Becky."

The man said, "I don't know who Becky is, but we'll help you find her."

Why would the man in black help him find her when he was the one who took her? Jeb's teeth ground together.

"This is your last warning, sir. Put down the knife."

Jeb smiled. Then he charged.

The man in black retreated, squeezing the trigger. Jeb didn't feel the bullets shred his chest as much as he heard the thunderous booms. He stopped in his tracks and his knife fell to the carpet. His hand didn't work anymore. He looked to his chest. Three tiny holes leaked blood onto his shirt. He touched his wounds. He looked to the man in black. A police officer now stood in his place.

The officer's face was twisted and distraught. A trickle of smoke trailed from the barrel of his gun and his hands trembled. "Sir, stay calm. I've got help on the way. Just get down on the floor. Please."

Jeb staggered backward onto the balcony. The officer lunged for him, but Jeb tumbled over the rail. Other than an initial jolt of pain when he struck the concrete sidewalk, he didn't feel anything, though he may have pissed himself.

A car squealed to a stop in the parking lot. Jeb looked around for the body of the man in black who should have fallen nearby, but he only saw police lights. Out of the corner of his eye, he saw one cruiser's door swing open.

A police officer leaped from the car and ran to him. She was pretty, her blond hair twisted into a bun. "Lay still, sir," she said, over and over. She dropped to her knees beside him. He felt her warm touch on his wrists and then felt the cold steel of her handcuffs. He didn't hear much of what she said when she shouted into her radio for medics. Jeb looked up at the morning clouds as they lumbered across the sky. *They are beautiful,* he thought. He shivered and looked around.

The police officer leaned closer and said, "Help is on the way, sir."

The other officer—the one who had shot him—appeared next to her. He was out of breath. "Get back," he shouted to the gathering crowd.

Someone shouted back, "Why'd you shoot that man?"

"Just stay back," he answered.

Someone else said, "I don't even see any weapons. Why'd you have to shoot him?"

Jeb stared at the sky again as the world slowed around him. Blood filled his mouth and he gagged on its bitter taste. When he tried to speak, crimson droplets sprayed the officer's white uniform shirt.

"Don't try to talk. Help will be here soon," she said.

"Where …" He choked and coughed. "… is the big man?"

"Who?"

"The man … who fell … before me."

"There was no one with you."

Why was she lying to him? "Your name?" he whispered between gasps for air.

"What?" she said. "Oh. Officer Mortin."

"No. Your first name."

She looked around like it was an odd request. Then she answered, "Becky. My name's Becky. Just be still."

Jeb chuckled and then coughed more blood onto her uniform shirt. "Becky," he said. "I love you."

She touched his shoulder. "You'll be all right. Just hold on."

The blue sky faded to a bright white until it was so bright that he couldn't see anymore. While police officers scrambled around him and sirens continued to wail in the distance, he heard music.

It was his favorite song. He smiled. *Johnny.*

END

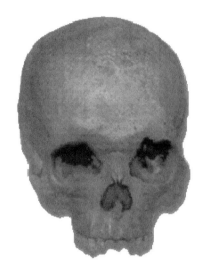

DEATH ALARM

"Those who cannot remember the past are condemned to repeat it." ~George Santayana

FIRST ALARM

Engine 22's air horn roared like a freight train. Though Ted couldn't imagine a tornado's rumble being louder, the sound hardly made an impact on the heavy rush hour traffic. Self-absorbed drivers cranked up their radios in their nearly soundproof Cadillacs and SUVs, failing to heed the warnings. Did they not hear, or did they just not care?

"Hey, rookie," Lieutenant Sanders shouted over the sirens. "You're on the knob if this is a fire."

Ted's heart beat faster than a frenetic heavy metal drum thrashing. *This could be the one. My first fire, and I get the nozzle.*

The dispatcher reported that the neighbor had heard the homeowner's smoke detector going off, which could mean anything from an actual fire to a false alarm. There was a nervous part deep within Ted, past the excitement and desire to get his first fire, that prayed for a false alarm. Ted thought he was ready— nine months of drill school told him he was—but with a real fire potentially right around the corner, he was having second thoughts. His hand trembled as he reached for his radio and stuffed it into the front holder on his bulky turnout coat.

The unconfident part of him wished they could just turn the truck around and return to the station. Hell, that part kind of wished he could go back to being a loan officer at the bank like before he had gotten a wild hair about being a fireman. At least at the bank he couldn't get burned. Robbed, maybe. But not burned. Of course, turning around wasn't an option. He slung his air bottle's awkward harness over his shoulders like a backpack and cinched it tight across his chest.

"You hear me, rook?" Sanders shouted from the front seat. "You're on the nozzle."

"Yeah, yeah, Lieu, I heard ya."

They pulled in front of a house straight out of a horror movie, complete with boarded windows and an overgrown front yard. A rusted-out Ford Mustang sat on blocks among the weeds. Probably a '68 or '69.

We're goin' in there?

The lieutenant barked into his microphone, "Engine Twenty-two's on the scene. Two-story residential. Nuttin' showin'. We'll investigate. Lieutenant Sanders has command."

Ted bounced from Engine 22 with such enthusiasm that he dropped his helmet.

Already walking toward the house, Sanders glanced back when he heard the helmet skitter across the gravel driveway. "Grab your lid, kid," he said with a grin.

The chauffeur, as firemen call their drivers, shot him a look that said, "Calm down." It was a look Ted was getting all too familiar with already in his short career. With a damn-the-calming-down zeal, he rushed to the back of the truck, yanked two hundred feet of fire hose from the hose bed, and lugged it to the front porch, nozzle in hand. He didn't hear an alarm.

Seeing the hose sprawled across the front yard, Sanders shook his head. Though his bushy gray mustache hid his upper lip, Ted still felt his sneer. "Did I tell you to pull that hose?" he asked.

Shit. Ted wilted like a kid who'd gotten an F on his test.

"A lot of hose to pick up for a fire alarm, kid." Sanders knocked on the front door. The throaty bark of a dog let loose inside. The lieutenant stood his ground.

The man who answered the door was wearing greasy jeans, a white T-shirt covered in stains, and faded prison-quality tattoos on both arms. He held a cigarette in his yellow-stained fingers. A grin revealed his two front teeth were missing, reminding Ted of the mythical tooth-to-tattoo ratio he had learned during his last shift. After helping a guy who had been shot six times yet was still talking, the older guys had joked that their district was full of overly tough sons of bitches. They said, "Around here, if someone has more tattoos than teeth, it seems nothing can kill them."

The homeowner didn't appear overly concerned at having the fire department show up at his front door. He spat a brown wad into the overgrown bush beside the porch. Some spit ran down his chin and he wiped it away with his forearm. "What do y'all want?" he shouted over the barking dog.

Ted looked past him to the kitchen where Cujo was raising all kinds of hell behind a flimsy child gate. If the beast simply realized the gate couldn't actually hold him back, Ted wasn't confident the skinny homeowner could either.

"Got a call that your fire alarm was going off," Sanders answered.

"From who? I ain't called you." He turned toward the barking dog and shouted, "Shut the hell up." The dog went silent. He turned back to Sanders. "Well, it ain't goin' off no more."

"Is everything good, then?" Sanders asked.

"I suppose. The alarm in the basement keeps going crazy. Prolly needs a new battery."

"Mind if we check it out?"

The man grinned again and stepped aside. "Be my guest." He pointed to the stairway. The house was a split level with half the stairs going up and the other half going down.

Sanders started in, but turned back. "Leave the hose, kid. We ain't gonna need it."

Ted dropped the nozzle on the porch and squeezed past the grinning homeowner to catch up to his boss. The basement was a dungeon with the only light coming from a tiny window and a dim forty-watter dangling from exposed wires in the farthest corner. It wasn't much help. Ted switched on the flashlight hanging from his coat. The lieutenant's light was already on, but it wasn't doing much good because it was quite charred and covered in soot.

Sanders pointed at the farthest wall. "Feel that drywall and make sure there's no heat behind it." Ted started across the floor when Sanders added, "And don't get all excited and put any holes in that wall, either.

Ted nodded and touched the wall with the back of his hand. "It's cool, Lieu."

"Yeah, that's what I figured. No heat means no fire behind it. Everything's fine down here. Let's go." He started back up the stairs, but paused and turned back. "Oh yeah, watch your step." He aimed his dull flashlight at the piles of dog shit littering the floor like landmines.

Ted lifted each foot to check the soles. Relieved, he carefully followed Sanders up the stairs. He was about to take the last step to the top landing when the hairs on the back of his neck stood on end and a chill ran the length of his spine like when his girlfriend touched him with her icy-cold fingers. He froze. It felt as though someone was watching him.

He spun with his flashlight. For a split second, he thought he saw the shape of a woman in the farthest corner of the basement, but as he focused she disappeared. He shook his head.

"Let's go, Ted," the lieutenant shouted from the front door. Ted took one last look into the basement and then hurried to the front porch.

He passed the homeowner. "Thank you, sir," he said.

The homeowner grunted. "Dog'll be out in five minutes. Get that shit off my lawn." He flicked his cigarette into the yard and then slammed the door closed.

Ted looked to the lieutenant with wide eyes.

Sanders grunted. "Don't worry about him. He's not going to do anything. All talk."

Ted started dragging the hose toward the back of the truck. He looked to Barry, the chauffer, who was standing with his hands on his hips. "What are you looking at me for? I didn't pull the hose." He chuckled and his belly bounced like Santa Claus's. Half the time he didn't even make a sound when he laughed, he just bounced. He headed to the driver's seat.

Ted looked to Sanders.

He shrugged. "What do you want me to do? Barry's cooking, and you know the cook runs the show." He started for the officer's seat.

"You're not going to help?" Ted called after him.

He paused and looked back with a grin. "I only help rookies load hose after they have four days out on company." He pulled his door closed.

Ted surveyed the spaghetti of hose and dropped his shoulders. *Damn.* It took some ingenuity and about twenty minutes, but Ted eventually got all two hundred feet of hose folded back into the bed. He was pouring sweat.

Neither Barry nor Sanders said much about his flub on the way back to the station, which Ted was grateful for. After all, what could they say? That Ted was a fool? He already knew that.

Back at the station, Ted stayed busy, mopping the floors, washing the trucks, and studying the three-ring binder of station procedures. It was important to stay busy as a rookie. That's when reputations were built. Once a firefighter got the knock of being lazy, it was hard if not impossible to shake.

Dinner was spaghetti. Ted loved spaghetti. He waited beside the kitchen island for the others to get their plates before daring to get his own. Being a rookie was tough sometimes. While an unwritten rule said he should start eating after the others, that same rule said he needed to be the first one doing the dishes. That meant he needed to eat fast.

As he reached for the pasta fork to serve himself, Barry cleared his throat. "Yours is by the sink," he said. Then his belly bounced.

Ted turned his head. A single line of noodles stretched from the sink to a larger pile. It looked almost like a tangled mess of fire hose. Ted grinned and bobbed his head. "I get it. Ha. Ha." He gathered the noodles onto his plate to the soundtrack of laughter. He only hoped they had washed the counter before they put his food on it.

SECOND ALARM

Ted's two days off were a welcome break from his constant nerves and the fear of making mistakes on the job. He began his next shift with an involuntary attempt at cooking breakfast for the guys. He wasn't much of a cook and told them so, but they didn't seem to care. They were hungry and he was the newest member, which meant he didn't have much choice.

They started their shift in the same way they had ended the last: hacking on Ted for his overzealous hose dragging incident. He struggled to not let their ribbing get under his skin, but he couldn't help being a little bothered. In the academy they had told him to find a sense of humor or the veterans would eat him alive, and he could already sense that they were right. If veterans didn't like a new guy, they'd ignore him, and that was far worse than the teasing. Ted was feeling pretty well-liked into his third shift.

While he was stirring the eggs, the station private phone rang in the other room. Someone else answered it. The door to the kitchen opened and Kelly stuck his head in. "Hey, Ted. Call for you."

"Thanks, Kelly."

"You know I'm not your secretary, right?"

"Yeah. Sorry. Can you stir these eggs for me?"

"I'm not your chef, either."

"I know. I'm sorry. I …"

Kelly brushed him off with a smile. "I'm just

kidding, kid. Go take your call. I've got this."

Ted raced to the small closet that had been converted into a phone booth. "Hello?" It was his girlfriend.

Her voice was a pleasant escape from the heckling. "Hi, sweetie," she said. "Clean up any hose yet today?"

Really? Her too? "Very funny."

"How's your day going?"

"Terrible. How the hell do you make pancakes?"

"You don't know how to make pancakes?"

"Less judging, more explaining. I don't have much time."

She started to tell him just as the kitchen door swung open. "Hey, kid," Lieutenant Sanders interrupted. "Your eggs are burning."

"Kelly said he'd stir them."

"Well, he's not."

Damn. "Honey, I gotta go. I'll call you back."

Before he joined the others in the kitchen, the long, steady fire tone blared over the PA. The crew poured through the door like someone had shouted, "Bomb."

Ted started to follow them to the truck, but Sanders grabbed his arm. "You wanna burn down the station?"

Ted stared slack-jawed at him.

"Your eggs?"

"Right. Sorry." Ted raced into the kitchen, turned off the burner, and removed the skillet. He hurried to the engine.

They were no sooner out the door when the lieutenant called back over the siren's wail, "Ah, damn. This is starting to get on my nerves." He glanced over his shoulder. "Three-two-five Riggs," he shouted as if the address should mean something to

Ted. When he saw that it didn't, he added, "The fire alarm from last shift? The one with the dog shit in the basement?"

"Oh yeah." Ted nodded while slipping his arms into his fire coat.

"No hose this time unless I tell ya. Got it?"

Ted nodded again.

The engine pulled up to the front of the familiar house. Once again, the lieutenant reported over the radio that there was "nuttin' showin'." He and Ted made their way to the open front door, only this time without the hose.

Unlike the last time, the alarm was screeching in the basement.

"Hello?" the lieutenant shouted over the barking dog behind the child gate.

The homeowner yelled from his out-of-sight upstairs perch, "Downstairs again. You know the way."

As Ted and Lieutenant Sanders climbed down the stairs, the homeowner shouted, "Shut up, mutt." His shout was followed by a loud clunk and a yelp.

Ted didn't see any smoke or signs that anything had been burning. "Another false, Lieu?"

Sanders grunted. "Probably. Go ahead and reset that alarm, kid. I'll go talk to the owner. This is getting on my nerves."

Ted continued down the stairs to where the smoke detector was mounted to a post at about eye level. After pressing the reset button on the detector and silencing the ear-splitting chirp, he shuffled back through the clothes and garbage and dog shit to the stairs.

But before he stepped onto the bottom step, another chill raced down his neck like it had on the shift before. He whipped his head around in time to see a woman dart past his flashlight beam and hide in the shadow of an old dresser. This time he knew he wasn't seeing things. He fumbled with his light and pointed it at her. The beam shone through her body as if she wasn't there.

"Hello?" Ted whispered. "Are you okay?"

She reluctantly stepped from the shadows. Her dark eyes invoked sadness unlike he had ever felt and he couldn't look away. She might have been the most beautiful person he had ever seen. He finally broke his gaze to look her over. Scabs and bruises wrapped her wrists.

She didn't walk so much as glide toward him. She was wearing a thin ivory nightgown that flowed behind her like streamers in the wind.

"Who are you?" he asked with a nervous quiver in his voice.

She reached out and touched his cheek. Her fingers were like ice. He shivered and stumbled backward. The sadness in her eyes reminded him of how his mother had looked when his father succumbed to cancer when he was eight. For some reason he wanted to cry.

She tilted her head and whispered, "Can you tell them about us? You must stop him."

Ted slowly nodded, despite not understanding a word.

"He did this to us." Her eyes drifted to the ceiling. "He'll do it to others if you don't tell them …" Her words trailed off and she jerked her head around as if someone had called her from behind. Her eyes narrowed. "You must go now," she insisted, terror replacing the sadness in her gaze.

"I don't understand."

She didn't answer as she backed toward the shadows.

"No, wait. What do you want me to tell them?"

"He knows I'm talking to you. You must go. You can't help us if you're not alive."

"Not alive? What do you mean? I want to help you."

As she floated past the smoke detector, she lightly blew into it, setting off another god-awful screech. Then she disappeared behind the dresser. Ted followed, but she was gone. On the floor behind the dresser, he noticed a four-by-four square of fresh concrete in the old, cracked floor.

The lieutenant appeared on the stairs with his fingers in his ears. "I told you to shut that damn thing off. What are you doing over there?"

"Sorry, Lieu. I'll get it." Ted rushed over and pressed the reset again. With his eyes locked on the shadowy corner, he slowly backed toward the stairs. The back of his heel banged the bottom step, almost tripping him up. He spun toward the landing where Sanders waited.

The crooked smile of the homeowner standing next to Sanders was a little creepy. "Don't be snoopin' around too much down there, kid. I don't want you to get lost." His eyes darkened and a scowl crossed his face. He lifted his gaze over Ted's shoulder toward the empty shadows on the other end of the basement. "Now, both of you get the fuck outta my house." His voice was gravelly and hard and serious. His creepy grin was miles gone.

Sanders flicked his wrist, motioning for Ted to follow him. "Then fix that detector," he said. Under his breath, he added, "Prick." Since Ted heard him, he was sure the man heard him, too.

At the top of the landing, Ted squeezed past the homeowner, who didn't try to move out of his way. "Excuse me," Ted said, but the man still didn't give him any extra room.

"Don't be coming back here," the man growled. "We don't need ya."

As they walked to the truck, Sanders asked, "What took you so long down there?"

"There's something weird about this place."

"Yeah. No kidding."

Ted glanced back at the homeowner standing in the doorway.

Sanders gave him an annoyed look and he stared coldly back. Sanders shouted, "Get that detector fixed. Or tell your neighbors to quit calling us when it goes off. We can't keep runnin' over here every shift."

The man spat brown gunk onto his siding and wiped his chin with his forearm. "I don't see why not. All you do is sleep, shit, and watch TV at the firehouse all day."

Ted expected an angry rebuttal from Sanders, but none came. Instead, Sanders rubbed his index finger and thumb along his bushy handlebar mustache and took a deep, calming breath. "Sir, you have a nice day." He forced a professional smile.

Ted caught up to him. "Hey, Lieu. I gotta tell you something."

Sanders climbed into the truck. Ted climbed into the jump seat behind him.

Sanders leaned around. "Yeah? What is it?"

"I saw something in the basement."

"Oh?"

Barry climbed in the driver's seat and shifted into gear.

"There's a woman down there."

"A woman? Hold up a minute, Barry. What do you mean?"

Barry stopped before they got going.

Ted wondered how best to explain what he saw. "She said she needed help."

Sanders's eyes widened. "I didn't see anyone. Why are you just now telling me this?" He opened his door to climb out.

"Wait, Lieu."

He stopped and turned back. "What?"

"Well, I don't … I mean … It wasn't exactly a regular woman."

Barry's eyes brightened. "This should be good."

Sanders sat back in his seat and leaned around to look at Ted. "What are you talking about, kid?"

"You're going to think I'm crazy."

"Too late."

"I think she was a …"

Sanders leaned forward, hanging on his words. "Go on."

There was no turning back now. "I think she was a ghost, Lieu." Ted cringed.

Sanders's shoulders slouched. Barry's gut bounced. Sanders turned back to the front and settled in his seat. He pointed through the windshield. "Home, Barry." He shook his head. "I'm still trying to figure you out, kid. Do you see ghosts often? Are you seeing any ghosts right now?"

Barry started for home.

Ted stared out the window as the houses zipped by. Maybe he shouldn't have said anything. Maybe he *was* going crazy. He had heard crazy sometimes came on when men were in their mid-twenties. He hoped he wasn't one of them.

THIRD ALARM

For the rest of the shift, Ted couldn't take his mind off the woman in the basement. She had seemed so real. The other firefighters had been surprisingly quiet about it, which meant they were planning something big. The rookie seeing ghosts wasn't going to just blow over. By the time he crawled into bed, the glowing red numbers on his alarm clock read 10:39 PM and he still hadn't heard a peep about seeing ghosts. He didn't get it. Why were they letting that slide? Unless he really was going crazy and they didn't know how to handle it.

He wished the lieutenant had seen her. They would believe *him*. The next time he looked at his clock, it read 1:13 AM. His eyes were finally heavy enough that he might get a few winks. His last thoughts were of the beautiful angel in the basement and wondering how he could have helped her.

The fire tones blared from the overhead PA and the lights of the bunkroom sparkled to life. The first thing Ted saw with his groggy eyes was his clock reading 3:07 AM. The PA reported a basement fire at 325 Riggs Drive. What was important wasn't what the dispatcher said, but what she didn't say. Specifically, the "alarm" part. The omission of that one word made all the difference in the world. Ted was the first one out of the bunkroom and beside the engine.

He leaped into his fire boots, pulled the suspenders over his shoulders, and was on the truck before he was awake enough to realize what the hell he was doing. His heart pounded against his breastbone like it owned a hammer.

Lieutenant Sanders jumped up front and smiled back at him. Ted wondered how he could be smiling.

The painfully slow door crept up and out of the way. Barry crushed the accelerator to the floor. The engine whined like a beast as the huge truck lurched forward like a snail.

The outside was a shaken snow globe. Ted shoved his arms into the sleeves of his fire coat and fastened the buckles along the front in spite of the jerking and jarring of the truck.

The fire engine's massive tires grabbed at whatever pavement they could find beneath the snow, but the truck still slid on its first turn off the station ramp. Ted didn't think twice about the poor conditions because he trusted Barry to safely get them where they were going. He was more worried about what they'd find when they got there.

He fidgeted with the straps of his air bottle and tugged them tight. With a shaky hand, he reached for a flashlight hanging from a hook and fastened it to a buckle on his coat.

Seeing his trembling hands, his partner that night, Marcus, shouted over the siren, "Nervous?"

"Just cold," he answered. But that was a lie.

He switched on his flashlight so he wouldn't forget. The truck turned onto Riggs Drive. Ted concentrated on slowing his breathing, but it didn't do any good. He was already winded. That feeling—that adrenaline rush—was what he'd heard so much about.

And he wasn't sure he liked it.

"Looks like a worker," Sanders shouted.

Ted was still getting used to all the firefighter shorthand, but he knew a worker, or working fire, meant there was a big fire and it was going to take a bit of work to extinguish.

This was it, Ted's first working fire.

"Ted, make sure you stay on my hip." Sanders started to turn back to the house, but paused and looked back again. "You can pull the hose this time."

Ted grabbed his helmet and wrested it onto his head. A million thoughts raced through his mind. Should he put on his mask now, or wait until he was at the front door? *What's the lieutenant doing? Okay. He's waiting.*

The engine stopped in front of the house he had become so familiar with recently. Thick, black smoke billowed from the shattered basement window. That meant the fire was hot. Lieutenant Sanders barked orders to the incoming companies over his radio.

Marcus shouted, "Gonna be a hot one," and Ted's gut instantly knotted. "Basement fires suck," Marcus added. "You get to the door and put on your mask. I'll feed you the hose line."

Ted nodded. He flung his door open. Thick snowflakes stuck to his mask then melted away as quickly as they had landed. The ground was slick and he had to be careful to keep his footing.

With the nozzle in hand, he dragged the hose to the front porch where Sanders was waiting with his mask on. Sanders shouted, "Remember, fast down the stairs. That'll be the hottest part."

Yeah. Like a chimney. That's what they said in the academy about basement fires.

Ted dropped to his knees and yanked the mask

straps over his head. He cinched them tight. Then he reached behind his back to open the valve on his air bottle. His next anxious breath sounded like Darth Vader on speed. After securing his helmet to his head with the chin strap and shoving his hands into his fire gloves, he nodded.

Lieutenant Sanders bashed the front door with an axe, shattering the frame. Smoke billowed through the opening. Ted started into the house, but the beast of a dog plowed through the doorway, almost knocking him over and scaring the piss out of him in the process. Luckily, the dog was more concerned with freedom than snacking on firemen.

"Slow your breathing, kid," Sanders reminded him.

They crawled through the front door and into the rolling black smoke. Before they started down the stairs, Sanders grabbed Ted's coat. "I hear someone upstairs. Wait here." He crawled into the hall, not slowed by the weight of the hose. After a few seconds, which felt more like hours, he shouted from the blackness, "Drop the hose, kid. We got one. Help me drag him out."

Ted dropped the nozzle and crawled through the smoke toward the lieutenant's voice. He felt along the floor until he found a pair of legs and grabbed hold. The guy barely felt like a person beneath the bulky gloves.

Sanders ordered, "On three. One. Two. Three."

They heaved the man's dead weight toward the steps in short bursts.

"Again," Sanders shouted.

Tug by tug, they lugged him down the stairs where Marcus grabbed him at the doorway and pulled him out.

Sanders grabbed Ted's shoulder strap, his masked

face inches away. "I'm going to finish the search. There might be more people. Don't go into the basement alone. Wait for me at the nozzle." He disappeared into the smoke.

Ted blindly swiped his hand along the floor until he brushed the hose and then followed it to the nozzle as ordered. Sanders seemed to be gone forever.

And then he heard a whisper that seemed to come from the basement. "He'll kiiiiill you," it moaned. "Run."

Ted perked up. "Lieu," he shouted.

Sanders didn't answer. If there was someone downstairs who needed him, they'd die if he waited any longer. He heard the sirens of incoming trucks, but they were still too far away. As he saw it, he had no choice. Water rushed from the truck to the nozzle. He bled the air from the hose through the doorway until water was flowing. Terrified, he inched his way into the black, smoke-filled stairwell.

The heat was blistering despite the protection of his turnout gear. He hugged the stairs as close as he could. As he dragged the hose down, the heat beat against him like he was crawling toward the sun. With each forward push it only got hotter. There was no relief. He considered retreating at least a dozen times. It was just too hot. His knees burned. His shoulders wilted under endless waves of torture.

From the basement, the voice cried, "Please. Don't come down here. That's what he wants."

"I won't leave you," Ted shouted back, his voice muffled behind his mask. This, he told himself, was what firefighters did. He wondered where Marcus had gone after dragging the victim to safety. He should have been helping with the hose. At the bottom of the steps, Ted shifted to the side and out of the chimney of the stairwell. The heat went from completely unbearable to slightly less so. Orange flickers danced within the billowing smoke. Ted glanced at the flashlight that should have been shining from his chest and saw nothing but blackness.

He pointed the nozzle at the source of the scorching heat and opened the bale. The water fell out and the hose went limp. *Oh no.* He had checked before going down like he was supposed to. He dropped the nozzle. "Where are you?" he shouted through his mask. "Come to my voice." He scooted along the floor, sweeping ahead with his gloved hands and shoving clothes and garbage and shit out of the way.

Through his gear, he felt a gentle touch on his shoulder and the world slowed. Though being so close to the fire should have been torturous, he barely felt the heat anymore. It was like an agonizing weight had just been lifted. The smoke twisted around him and then parted like the Red Sea. His flashlight beam finally cut through. It was as if someone had flipped a switch and Ted was suddenly all-aware. His nerves, his fears, his apprehensions—all gone. He wondered if that was what happened when a person died. Or became a real firefighter.

"You shouldn't have come down here," his angel whispered.

He turned to her. She moved with the fluidity of a ripple of water. An overwhelming sense of calm washed over him.

"We gotta get outta here," he said.

She sadly shook her head. "It's too late now. He's won again." Following her words was a rumble that filled the stairwell. Part of the upper floor crashed down onto the stairs. Ted flinched, but he was unable to break his gaze from hers.

She touched his cheek through his mask. "I didn't mean for it to end like this."

"Why did you call us earlier? What did you want us to do?"

"I wanted you to tell the world what he did to us. I wanted you to stop him from killing again."

"Then come with me. I'll get us out of here somehow. We'll tell the world together."

"No. I'm so sorry, Ted. There is no way out."

"Bullshit."

She stepped to the side. Two more women and a little girl appeared at the farthest wall, flames gyrating around them. Ted's angel tilted her head with a sad smile. The four spirits looked toward the rubble blocking the stairs.

"Your friends are trying to find you. I'm so sorry, but they won't reach you in time. I can't hold the heat back any longer. You must warn them about him before he kills them, too."

Sanders's muffled voice called from the landing beyond the debris, "Ted. We're coming."

Ted's angel leaned in and kissed his cheek through his mask. "I will see you soon," she whispered. A single tear wet her cheek as she backed up to stand with the others. Smoke oozed into the clearing between them until they disappeared.

Ted's flashlight beam vanished within the smoke again. The heat closed in—scorching and hotter than he'd ever felt before. His every movement caused his arms and legs to press against the inside of his gear, and it burned like a hot water surge in the shower. His low air alarm chirped and then began to ring. The air from his bottle heated and burned his mouth and throat. He crawled to the bottom of the stairs and heaved at a wooden I-beam blocking the way. He'd have to lift half the house to even have a chance.

He screamed, "Lieu. Lieu." He pulled and clawed at rubble, but it was too high and too thick. His shoulders and the back of his neck blistered through his gear.

"We're coming, kid," Sanders shouted back.

"No. You don't understand. It's too late for me. The guy. He's a k—"

"It's okay, kid. We got him out. He's safe."

Ted ripped at broken drywall and splintered wood. "No, Lieu. You don't understand."

The lieutenant either ignored him or didn't hear. "We're coming for you, kid. The fire's in the walls. This whole place is coming down."

"No. Wait. Listen to me. The guy that you rescued. He's a—"

"No time, kid. Save your air. We're gettin' you out."

The ceiling rumbled. When Ted looked up, what felt like the weight of a car slammed his shoulders and crushed him to the ground, knocking the wind out of him. Something hot, maybe a gas pipe, pressed against his leg and instantly scorched his skin through his gear. He'd never heard anything like the muffled cry that left his mouth.

A chainsaw screamed from the floor above at the opposite end of the basement. He tried to move his arms, but the weight was too crushing. He grunted and strained against it, but it only tired him more. His low air alarm kept ringing, a constant reminder that he was going to die.

The crack of axes against wood and the screech of chainsaws ceased long enough for Sanders to shout, "We're coming, kid. Hold on." His voice sounded miles away, and it might as well have been. The racket began again.

Ted was surprised when an overwhelming sense of serenity—some might call it resignation—settled in. His breathing calmed. Even the high-pitch squawk of his firefighter-down alarm didn't rattle him like it should.

It won't be long now.

The ring of his low air alarm wound down like a dying alarm clock.

Ding ... Ding ...... Ding .... Ding .... And then nothing.

His angel appeared beside him, knelt down, and held his hand. She sobbed.

His mask sucked to his face, empty of air like a plastic bag over his head. His eyes bulged.

"You can rest now," she whispered.

He slowly faded.

NEW ALARM

Cindy spent the first part of her first shift sweating over the stove cooking breakfast for the crew at Station 15. She fancied herself quite the cook and couldn't wait until they tasted her famous pepper jack eggs.

"Hey, newboy," Harold shouted from the table. "How're the eggs coming along? I'm starvin' over here."

All rookies were called "newboy" regardless of gender, but the way Harold said it made Cindy suspect he was a misogynistic dinosaur. She bit her tongue, knowing she couldn't get away with ripping him a new one until she had better proven her worth around the station. The last thing she needed was to piss off one of the veterans and get herself a bad name right out of the gate. Maybe she could be less forgiving on day two. "Almost ready, sir."

He said, "Damn rookies. Slower than death. We'll probably get a run before we even get to eat." Then he mumbled, "You'd think a woman would be more useful in the kitchen."

Yep. Dinosaur.

Cindy couldn't help but wonder how many meals her tormentor had actually missed in his distinguished career; the struggling buttons on his uniform shirt indicated it hadn't been many. Cindy served the rest of the crew like a good rookie should and then sat down across from Harold for her own bowl of eggs.

Harold crammed a forkful into his mouth. "Let me tell ya a story, girl. You ever heard about the rookie down at Twenty-two's?"

Cindy stirred a pinch of salt into her mound of eggs. She nodded. Everyone had heard the story. It was brought up almost daily at the academy.

"Well, you're gonna hear it again. It's important that all you young kids know this story in and out. Did they show you the memorial display?"

"Yeah." The whole class had taken a tour of the station on the day they told Ted's story.

"You don't want them to make one like that for you."

No kidding.

"It was three years ago. This newboy named Ted was working his second or third shift, I can't remember which, when he got himself a real shit-kicker of a basement fire. The engine crew had a pretty good rescue that day, but for heaven only knows why, that rookie …," he trailed off and rubbed his chin, deep in thought. "I can't believe it's been three years already. Anyways, for some god-forsaken reason that rookie left his lieutenant and went into the basement on his own. That's when the whole first floor came down on him." He sighed and shook his head. "It was a damn shame, is what it was."

The salt-and-pepper-haired veteran—more salt than pepper—shoveled eggs onto his toast, wrapped it like a sandwich, and then continued his tale. "The rest of that boy's crew tried to get him out …" A chunk of egg rocketed from his mouth onto Cindy's wrist. She tried not to acknowledge the projectile. Meanwhile, the old-head didn't miss a beat. "They might have gotten to him, too, but—and now this is the crazy part—that's when the guy living in the house—the very guy they had rescued—started sticking them with a knife. It turned out he had poked a bunch of holes in the rookie's hose. Then he snuck up on the lieutenant and jammed a knife in his back. That monster stabbed Twenty-two's entire crew that day. Left 'em for dead. I think the chauffer lost an eye. They're lucky they didn't all die like Ted."

The kitchen door swung open and Jacob strolled in.

Jacob was a good-looking guy who didn't have much more time on the department than Cindy, but he still couldn't resist giving his own ribbing. "These eggs better be good, rookie."

Rookie? He's got like a year on me, if that.

Captain Rudolph, a grey-haired man who reminded Cindy of her own father, followed Jacob through the door. He was a gruff and quiet man, but had warmth in his smile.

Harold swiped his sleeve across his face, smearing chewed-up egg on his uniform, and hollered, "Hey, Cap. I'm just telling her about the Twenty-two house story."

The captain grunted. He scooped a plateful of eggs. "The eggs look good, Cindy," he said.

"Thanks, Cap."

Harold continued, "All those guys retired after that, and I can't say I blame them. It was a real mess. That Marcus guy lost a lung."

He stopped cramming food into his yap long enough to turn to the captain. "I don't know what they were doing, but you don't have to worry 'bout me, Cap. Anyone comes at you in a bad way, I'll take care of it." He shook his fist like a UFC fighter.

Rudolph grunted again and smirked, not impressed.

"And the guy that did it was never caught, right?" Cindy asked, though she knew the answer. Everyone did.

"Nope. He ran off when he heard more sirens coming. But before he did, he did a number on the poor lieutenant's face. Cut him up real good. Put him in the hospital for a month. You couldn't recognize him, they say. At least, not till after the surgeries. I never knew the guy before, but I went to the hospital just the same. I tell ya, he was a mess. Lost a kidney, and I think he was left with one of those shit-bags for a while, too. He moved to Florida or somewhere sunny after it all. Hey, Cap, did you know him?"

"Um-hm."

Harold smacked Cindy's shoulder. "Let that be a lesson to ya, girl."

"Yeah? What's that?"

He crammed his last mouthful of eggs into his mouth. "Don't go into fires," he said, and almost spat his eggs out laughing at his own cleverness.

Cindy forced an uncomfortable chuckle. Before she could think of a witty retort, the fire tones interrupted breakfast. Excited, she raced to the engine. Nothing like getting your first fire right out of the gate. Harold hopped in the driver's seat and the engine roared from the station.

They pulled up to a one-story house at the end of a short driveway. A man was standing by his mailbox at the end of the drive. He was barefoot and shirtless and smoking a cigarette. Light smoke drifted from an open basement window.

Rudolph looked back and said, "Pull the hose." Then he climbed out.

"My kid's in there," the homeowner said emotionlessly as he met the captain at the side of the truck.

"Where?" Rudolph asked urgently.

"I don't know. I think the little brat might have been playing with matches downstairs."

"We'll find him." Rudolph directed the man to wait with Harold next to the engine pump. Axe in hand, he headed for the house. Cindy grabbed the hose line and raced to catch up. Within seconds, Rudolph put his mask on and disappeared through the front door.

Cindy knelt on the porch and slipped on her mask. "Cap?" she shouted into the house.

The piercing shriek of a smoke detector drowned out her voice, along with any answer Rudolph might have given. She crawled through the first room, keeping one hand on the wall like she had learned in training. "Cap," she shouted again. "Where are you?"

In the smoky maze of the cluttered house, Cindy found an open door with a set of steps descending into the smoke. A firefighter-down alarm screeched from below. She pulled the hose down the stairs. "Cap? Are you all right?" she shouted.

In the center of the basement, next to a dead dog, Rudolph knelt on the floor surrounded by smoke and flames. A cocoon of clear air encircled him. He stared at the blank wall.

"I'm coming, Cap." Cindy opened the nozzle and blasted the fire with a mule kick of water. She whipped the hose around like she'd learned and darkened the flames. They were nearly out when the hose went suddenly limp and the rush of water reduced to a trickle.

"Cap, something's wrong with the hose."

Rudolph didn't move, still staring forward. His firefighter-down alarm still wailed. Cindy threw the worthless hose to the side as the flames started to grow again. She hurried to Rudolph's side.

Cindy grabbed the captain's arm. "Cap, what are

you doing?" She reset his alarm so she could better hear. Then she punched the shrieking smoke detector mounted to a post to shut it up as well. "Cap, what's going on?"

Rudolph stayed frozen, gazing into the smoke. "Did you see her?" he finally asked, as calm as a summer breeze despite the smoke growing thicker and blacker.

"See who, Cap? We gotta get out of here."

"The angel," he answered. "She said we shouldn't have come here."

"What are you talking about?"

"You should go before it's too late, Cindy."

Cindy pulled on his shoulder. "What about you?"

Rudolph pulled back. He turned toward her and tilted his head. "You don't expect me to leave her, do you?"

"There's no one there, Cap. Come on."

Pieces of flaming debris fell around them.

Cindy yanked the captain toward her with everything she had, sending them both to the floor. The impact jarred something loose in Rudolph. He shook his head, dazed. "What's happening?" he asked.

Cindy grabbed his coat with both hands and screamed, "We gotta go."

Rumbling in the ceiling announced a pending collapse. Cindy panicked. She scrambled toward the stairs with Rudolph on her heels. They reached the staircase as the ceiling shifted and fell. The sound of a train roared through the basement. Cindy flinched away.

But the ceiling didn't crush her. She slowly turned back.

There was another firefighter standing in full gear

midway up the stairs. Cindy didn't recognize him.

"Go," the firefighter shouted as he strained to hold up the weight of the entire house. His arms quivered and his face twisted in pain.

Cindy froze.

"Get outta here. I can't hold it much longer."

Cindy climbed the stairs, stopping when she got to him.

The firefighter screamed, "What are you waiting for? Keep going."

"You're blocking the way. I can't get around you."

"Go through me."

Cindy looked crazily at him.

"Do it."

Cindy charged forward with her eyes closed and passed right through her savior as if he wasn't there. From the top landing, she turned back in time to see Rudolph pass through him as well.

Once they were both on the landing, the firefighter shouted, "You have to stop him."

"Who are you?" Cindy cried.

"I worked at Twenty-two's."

Cindy tilted her head. "Ted?"

Ted smiled at her over his shoulder. And then part of the first floor crashed down on him.

Rudolph grabbed Cindy's arm and screamed, "Grab my boot and keep up with me." Crawling, they strafed what was left of the floor through the growing inferno until they saw daylight through the open front door. They scrambled onto the porch with flames licking their backs.

Cindy lifted her head to the engine where Harold and Jacob knelt on the homeowner next to the front bumper. The man was unconscious and bleeding from the temple. Harold appeared winded and was holding an axe.

Rudolph stood up and ripped off his mask. Cindy followed his lead. The heat from behind was scorching.

Harold shouted, "Cap, this son of a bitch tried to stab us after I caught him poking holes in your hose. I had to knock his skinny ass out. Are you guys okay?"

Rudolph nodded. He keyed his mic and called for the police to be dispatched to their location on an emergency. He reached back and tapped Cindy's shoulder as additional firetrucks arrived on the scene. "You did real good in there," he said.

"Should we try and put out the fire?"

Rudolph looked to the flames leaping from every window. "Nah. There's nothing we can do for it. After the police get here and we don't have to worry about that psychopath anymore, we can throw some water on it for appearances, but it's a total loss. We just need to keep that guy from hurting anyone."

When word got out about what had happened, the situation quickly escalated into a media circus. News vans lined the road and cameramen set up their cameras. Early reports from the detectives on scene pointed to something much larger than a simple house fire.

Whispers started to spread of similarities between this fire and the tragic murder of Ted and the horrific wounding of the others a few years back.

Rudolph and Cindy sat on the back bumper of Engine 15 and sipped some water while waiting for their turn to talk to the detectives.

"Can you believe what just happened, Cap?" Cindy asked.

"I don't know what to believe."

"Are you going to tell them about Ted?"

Rudolph grunted. "I'm not sure what to tell them. I'm not even sure what I saw."

"But you did see him, right? I'm not going crazy, am I?"

"I saw something. I'm not sure it's something I want to try and convince these detectives of, though. At least, not until I have a bit of time to think more about it."

"Yeah. Me neither."

A detective approached. Cindy tossed her empty water bottle into the homeowner's dumpster and headed down the driveway to meet him. She glanced back at Rudolph. He rubbed his forehead. Then he gave her a reassuring nod. She shook the detective's hand.

"Quite the day, huh?" the detective said.

"Hmph. You don't know the half of it."

END

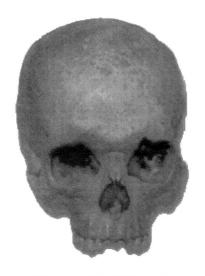

CATCHTIME

"Whatever is begun in anger ends in shame."
~ Benjamin Franklin

I
THEN

JD had always struggled with his temper. Though he'd never seriously hurt anyone, he had been kicked out of school for fighting more times than he could count on one hand. After graduation, he had lost his first two jobs for arguing with his bosses. Punching the second one probably wasn't the best way to express his feelings.

At twenty-three, he was working construction and making a decent living. Enough that he was able to buy his dream car, a brand new 2010 Chevy Camaro. Fire engine red with matte-black racing stripes and ball-busting eighteen-inch wheels. It was a beauty. He put a couple thousand miles on it right away just cruising and taking unnecessary trips to the store. He followed each of those trips with a good washing and never took his beast out in the rain.

His beater car, a 1996 Grand Am, was his everyday car. That's the car he took to work. He didn't want to risk the Camaro's paint job in the dirty parking lot full of beat-to-hell pickup trucks the other guys drove.

But that day the forecast promised warm temperatures with not a cloud in the sky. It seemed a crime not to drive his Camaro on such a nice day. Plus, it was his day to take Freddy home from work and he had been itching to show Freddy his car.

Freddy was a nice old hillbilly who worked harder

than anyone JD had ever met. On JD's third day on the job Freddy had sliced his hand wide open on a thin piece of sheet metal that cut right through his worn-out gloves. There was blood everywhere. While JD momentarily froze in shock, Freddy calmly tied a handkerchief around his hand and cinched it tight. When he noticed JD watching, he lifted a bloody finger to his lips and smiled. Most of the guys figured Freddy didn't want Foreman Steve or OSHA to catch wind of it because it might shut down the site for a bit. But JD later learned Freddy was more concerned about the mandatory alcohol and drug tests that came after injuries.

That was part of the reason Freddy needed a ride. As hard-working as he was, he was also quite the drunk. The others joked that Freddy never missed a day of work or a shot of vodka. He'd lost his license and lived twenty minutes' drive away, so the others sometimes gave him a ride. On the days no one offered, that hard-working bastard rode his bike. Even in the winter. He had to leave his house at four in the morning to make it on time.

JD knew how much Freddy liked muscle cars. He often pointed them out whenever one drove by the site. JD parked in the back of the lot, taking up two spots just to avoid any potential door dings.

At the end of the shift, JD stood in line to dust off his clothes with the air compressor. He desperately hoped Freddy would do the same before getting into his Camaro. Then he saw Freddy heading toward the parking lot and his heart sank. He had to think quick. "Hey, Freddy," he shouted, and waved him over.

Freddy grinned and then coughed a two-pack-a-day cough before lighting up a fresh smoke. He took a swig from his thermos, and JD could guess what was in it.

JD used the air hose to blow the dust from his clothes and then directed it at Freddy, who looked like Pigpen from Peanuts when the air hit him. To JD's dismay, Freddy walked away before he was finished. JD hurried to catch up.

Freddy asked, "So, where's this legendary ride you've been telling everyone about?"

JD waited until his car was in view and gave a subtle nod toward it. He peeked at Freddy's face for his reaction. Freddy didn't disappoint. His eyes widened. He slowed and side-eyed JD. "That's yours?" he asked. Then he bobbed his head approvingly.

JD grinned.

"Well, I'll be. I might just let you take me home every day, kid. Should I just strap my bike to the roof?"

JD's brain skipped. He stuttered, "Uh ... I'm ... Uh ..."

Freddy gave him a light jab with an elbow to the side. "Calm down. I'm just kidding. I'll need a ride tomorrow morning if I leave my bike here, though."

"Sure. I can do that."

Freddy tossed his finished cigarette butt before pulling out a fresh one. He held it between his teeth while he searched his pockets for a lighter.

JD shook his head. "No smoking in the car. Cool?"

Freddy shrugged and put the cigarette back in the pack. Then he took another swig from his thermos. Once he sat in the car and took in the interior with a swooping gaze, he marveled, "This thing's like a cockpit."

JD smiled. "Put on your seatbelt."

Freddy scoffed. "Seatbelts are for sissies."

"You ready?"

"Kid, I was born ready."

JD really got on it pulling out of the lot, leaving two long, black streaks on the pavement and plenty of smoke. Freddy held on to both sides of the seat, his seatbelt alarm beeping every few seconds. JD hoped he'd get the hint, but as annoying as the alarm was, Freddy wasn't moved to buckle up.

"How fast can you get this thing going?" Freddy asked.

"Wait till we get on the freeway and you'll see."

But getting to the freeway became more of a chore than anticipated when JD pulled behind a slow beater of a pickup truck overflowing with scrap metal. The rusted tailgate was held on by a leather strap and looked to be a bump away from falling off completely.

JD drifted slightly toward the double yellow lines, but the other lane wasn't clear enough to pass. The old Dodge truck had a bumper sticker that said "BACK OFF" in bold black letters. Below that in smaller print it said "Not responsible for anything that hits your car if you ride too close."

JD rolled his eyes and drifted to the double yellow again. The path still wasn't clear. He was itching to give Freddy a real ride. He twisted his grip on the steering wheel in pent-up anticipation like it was a motorcycle throttle. "Look at that," he groaned, pointing at the bumper sticker. "Can you believe that jackass? He thinks a bumper sticker makes him immune if something falls from his truck and—"

Just as he said it, the beater truck hit a bump and a fist-sized piece of jagged metal toppled from the pile. JD's eyes bulged and he tried to swerve without moving into oncoming traffic. The hunk of metal glanced off the front of his Camaro before he lost sight of it. He could hear it bouncing horribly along the undercarriage. The blood drained from JD's face. His stomach turned.

Freddy chuckled. "You believe that shit? You were just saying that if—"

"Shut up, Fred." JD suddenly couldn't see straight. Images of his front end hanging by a thread flashed through his mind. A cruise missile exploded in his stomach, filling him with angry fire. He hadn't felt such rage in years. He saw gouged red paint and dents everywhere he looked. "Hold on." He stomped on the gas pedal.

Freddy finally put on his seatbelt.

JD jerked the wheel and the Camaro shot into the oncoming lane, causing an SUV to veer onto the berm and lay on the horn. The Camaro pulled alongside the truck. An old man sat in the driver's seat, his head barely higher than the steering wheel. JD swerved aggressively toward him, but the old man didn't seem to notice. Or care. JD gunned it, swerved in front of the truck, and then jammed on his brakes. The old man stopped inches from his back bumper.

JD snarled, "I'm gonna fuck him up."

2
NOW

Daniel stood in Maddy's she-shed as she sat in front of her computer. It was her big moment. The one she had worked so hard toward.

"I don't know, honey. Are you sure I'm ready?" Maddy asked.

Daniel was sure. He had been pushing her to start her own craft business almost since the first time they'd met. She had been holding a coffee mug she had decorated herself with her own art. It was a drawing of a tiny yellow bird crafting a sculpture out of its nest. It became her logo and now adorned business cards, stationary, her website, and anything else she could stick it on. In a way, that little bird had started their three-year love affair that was still going strong.

"Do you really think someone will want a mug with my doodles on them?" Maddy never trusted her own talent, and her lack of confidence sometimes drove Daniel nuts. Few people he knew had as much talent as her.

She hesitated. Though everything was ready—the website, the price list, a half-dozen designs, and two boxes of blank white mugs—she feared pressing the confirm button. All she needed now were customers. And confidence.

Daniel knew a post on the social media site

CatchTime would get her family and friends to buy something, but he didn't want charity to be the reason she succeeded. He wanted her first sale to be to a complete stranger. That was the only way to convince her she was good enough. So, as a gift, he purchased a hundred dollars of ad space on CatchTime. People all around the country who had listed crafts as an interest would hopefully see Maddy's logo. And, if all went well, click on her site. And, if all went *really* well, buy some loot.

She sat in front of the computer with her finger hovering over the mouse. One simple click and she'd put herself in front of the world, "naked" as she called it. She looked up as Daniel crowded her shoulder.

He chuckled. "Well?"

She chuckled back. "I'm afraid."

The silliness of being afraid to push a mouse button struck them both at the same time and their chuckles turned into outright laughter.

Daniel asked, "What's the worst that can happen? Everyone stops drinking coffee all of a sudden?" He reached beneath her hand and rested his finger on the mouse button. "Should I?"

Maddy squeezed her eyes shut, held her breath, and pushed his finger against the mouse. Click.

A message popped up on the screen: *Your ad has been enhanced.*

Maddy sighed and melted into her chair. One would have thought she'd run a marathon.

Daniel put a hand on her shoulder. "Now we just wait for the orders to flood in."

She leaned her cheek against his hand. "Let's just start with one and see where it goes."

They watched the screen as if it held all the answers to the mysteries of the universe and even a blink would make them disappear. "Should I hit refresh?" she asked.

"I think it refreshes itself … Doesn't it?"

"I don't know. Maybe I'll just refresh it once." As she reached for the mouse, a chime sounded and an orange smiley face flashed in the upper left corner and startled her. Her flinch made her start laughing again.

Daniel smirked. "You're jumpy. Go on. Click it."

She clicked the smiley face and it brought up a comment from someone named Barbara. *Love your design! How can I get one?*

Maddy's eyes widened. "What should I tell her?"

"Have her go to the website."

"Right." Maddy typed what Daniel suggested.

A blue smiley face almost instantly popped up, indicating she had a reply from Barbara. *Thanks*, it read.

Daniel rubbed her shoulders. "I guess now we just wait, huh?"

"I guess."

Maddy's first sale came in around 8:00 that night. It was for a coffee mug covered in glitter with the phrase "First, Coffee. Then Children."

Maddy and Daniel celebrated with a glass of wine. Three glasses, actually.

Maddy sold three mugs overnight. It wasn't quite the firestorm they had hoped for, but one of the purchases came from someone who had heard about it from a friend, so that was something.

Daniel did his part for his wife's business at the office building where he worked. He made sure to carry his custom mug that read "Real architects build it right the first time" whenever he was on the sixth floor. It was the company motto. A guy named Rich had showed some interest when Daniel brought it the first time, so Daniel made a note to tell him they were for sale now.

That morning's coffee had gone right through him and Daniel struggled to make it to his lunch break. He spent the first part of his break teaching the toilet bowl an angry lesson. Despite his curtesy flush, he dreaded anyone else coming in for the next few minutes. While he sat on the toilet, he pulled out his phone.

He opened the stock market app first. "Figures," he whispered. "Up another two bucks." Daniel had a stock market problem. Though he was pretty good at picking stocks, he was never able to pull the trigger and buy them. No matter how much he liked a company, he was terrified of losing money. Every time a stock he was interested in went down, he felt relieved he hadn't invested. And every time a stock went up, he felt like a cowardly idiot.

"Look at that. Ford up too. Another buck." It drove him nuts. He swiped out of the market app and logged into Maddy's CatchTime account for a peek. He no longer used CatchTime himself because he struggled too much to get past the negative comments strangers sometimes posted. Heck, even when people tried to be nice, they were often oblivious to how they came across. It got to him so much that if he hadn't deleted the app when he did, he would have gotten himself in trouble.

He clicked on Maddy's business page to see how she was doing. Four unread smiley faces. He clicked on one. It was an order for three Christmas mugs. He pumped his fist. "Way to go, babe," he whispered.

Then he clicked the next smiley face. It was from someone named Jerry. His comment was only a sentence long, but one word immediately stuck out: *Bitch*. Daniel shook his head, stunned. It took him a couple seconds to refocus and read the whole comment. *Your art is shit, Bitch.*

Daniel's stomach twisted. He couldn't believe it, so he read it again.

Your art is shit, Bitch.

It was a horse kick to the gut. He studied each word in case he had read it wrong. It didn't make sense that someone could be so mean. What was it about social media that let people be such assholes? How dare this "Jerry" be so—

The bathroom door squeaked open.

Daniel shook away the frustration, closed the app, and shoved his phone in his pocket. He finished his business, washed his hands while someone from the office stood at the urinal, and hurried to the breakroom for his lunch. He hoped Maddy hadn't seen Jerry's comment.

Daniel dumped his paper bag on the table in the empty break room. There was a turkey sandwich, a container of cinnamon applesauce, a spoon, and a bag of nacho chips. He bought a root beer from the vending machine and sat down. Beneath the baggie holding his sandwich was a small slip of paper. He loved when Maddy sent a note along with lunch. He flipped it over. "Have a great day! Love, Maddy." Her bird logo was neatly printed in one corner, which made him think of the nasty comment from Jerry again. He wished he could get over little things like that easier. He stuffed the note into his back pocket. He kept all her notes. To a guy like Daniel, letters and notes and mementos meant the world.

A guy named Charlie soon entered for a soda. Daniel poured his root beer into his coffee mug in case Charlie stopped for a chat. It might make him a shill, but anything for a sale, right? When Charlie nodded to him and headed for the door with soda in hand, Daniel called out, "Hey, Charlie."

Charlie turned back. "What's up, Daniel?" Though Charlie was considered the best architect in the firm, no one wanted to talk to him much because his chronic bad breath would turn away a skunk. Combined with his eternally half-tucked shirt and stained pants, Charlie didn't seem concerned about how he came across to people.

Daniel, however, enjoyed talking to him because Charlie didn't think he was better than everyone else, unlike some of the other guys in the office.

Before Charlie even sat down across from Daniel, his breath wafted by. It was particularly rank that day—garbage out in the sun kind of rank. Daniel offered him a stick of gum and, to his delight, Charlie accepted.

"What's up, Daniel?"

"My wife started a business and—"

"How is Maddy anyways? We sure miss her here at the office."

"Oh, she's good. I wasn't sure we could afford her quitting her day job, but we've tightened some strings and it's working out."

"It was always nice seeing her smiling face when I came in. That girl they've got down at the information desk now isn't so friendly. She barely smiles."

"I'll tell Maddy you said that."

"Please do. So, what do you need? I've got a

meeting in a few minutes."

"Do you use CatchTime?"

"What's that? Social media?"

Daniel nodded.

"I don't use any of that stuff. Why?"

"Well, it's just this comment somebody left for Maddy's new business. Look at this." Daniel pulled up Maddy's CatchTime account on his phone and showed Charlie Jerry's comment.

Charlie shrugged his shoulders. "What do you care what …," he looked closer with a squint, "… Jerry says? Who the hell is Jerry?"

"I don't know. Just some stranger, I guess."

"I wouldn't worry about it. Did you see that 60 Minutes report on social media?"

Daniel shook his head.

"It was about trolls. There are people who just talk crap on the internet for attention. Ignore Jerry. He's probably a troll."

"Yeah. I guess. It just sticks in my craw."

"You gotta let things like that go, man. Some people just try and get a rise out of others." Charlie looked at his watch. "Is that all you wanted?"

Daniel nodded.

Charlie stood up. "Hey, tell Maddy I'll take one of those mugs with the company motto on it. I've been meaning to ask for one after I saw you carrying it the other day."

Daniel lifted his mug and tapped the side. "Ten bucks, free delivery."

"Yeah. That's the one." Charlie pulled out his wallet and tossed a ten on the table.

Daniel smiled. "Thanks, Charlie. I'll see you tomorrow."

Charlie grinned as he walked toward the exit. He

stopped and turned back. "Hey, do you know where there's any deodorizing spray? Someone stunk up the bathroom big time."

Daniel cringed. "I'll see if I can find some." He finished his sandwich and cleaned up his area. Before he went back to work, he pulled out his phone and read Jerry's message one more time. He shook his head. Charlie was probably right. Jerry was a troll. He'd be wise to let it go.

3
THEN

JD flung his door open almost before his car was in park and leaped out in a fury.

Freddy scrambled from the passenger side. "JD, calm down," he shouted.

JD barely heard him. He sprinted to the front of his Camaro and surveyed the damage. There was a quarter-sized dent with a nice chip in the paint next to the driver's-side fog light.

The old man climbed out of his truck. "Hey, kid," he shouted. "What the hell you tryin' to do? Give me a heart attack?"

JD lifted his eyes. Instead of seeing the man, he saw a big red dent in the man's forehead. His face burned with anger. *Calm down,* he told himself repeatedly as he walked toward the truck. The old man wore overalls and had plenty of grease on his hands. He even had a picturesque smudge of grease across his cheek. He spat tobacco to the side.

Through clenched teeth JD said, "Something fell out of your truck and hit my car." It took everything he had to not punch the man. Especially when the man smirked at him.

"Well, what do you want me to do 'bout it?"

"You're gonna pay to fix it."

The old man pulled out his empty pockets. Then he scratched his ass. "I ain't got no money." He nodded toward his scrap pile. "You want a piece of metal instead?" He snickered.

JD didn't see the humor. His fists tightened at his sides.

Then the old man pushed his luck. "Besides, it ain't my problem you can't drive worth shit. You read the bumper sticker, right?" He snort-laughed.

A bolt of lightning shot up from JD's feet and into his hand. The next thing he knew, his fist was plowing into the side of the man's head.

Freddy sprang forward and grabbed JD's arm, but he was too late. "What are you doing?" he shouted as he pulled JD away.

The old man fell backward, smacking his head against a rock. He was instantly unconscious.

Freddy gave JD a hard shove toward his car and then ran to the old man's side. Another car had stopped and the lady driving held a cell phone to her ear. Freddy knelt beside the old man, who started to seize.

JD went to his car and leaned against the trunk. He seethed as he watched.

Freddy looked up with wide eyes. "I don't think he's breathing anymore," he shouted.

"Good," JD mumbled to himself. "That's what he gets."

Several cars pulled onto the berm and a crowd started to form. Distant sirens approached. Freddy didn't appear to know CPR, but he pressed on the old man's chest with both hands just the same. A guy from the crowd said he knew first aid and squatted beside Freddy. He took over with what looked more like the CPR JD had seen on TV.

The guy continued rhythmically pressing on the old man's chest until the emergency squad arrived and the medics took over. A police officer arrived around the same time. The lady with the cell phone stood talking to the officer, but she was too far away for JD to hear what she said. Then she pointed at him.

As JD's rage slowly subsided and the cop approached, his stomach turned a little. It felt strange because it wasn't for the reasons he might expect. While he knew he should feel bad seeing the old man dying on the side of the road, for some reason he didn't. His stomach turned because he was starting to realize the potential consequences of his actions. "Is he dead?" he asked coldly.

The officer looked to the working paramedics and shouted, "Hey, Elliot. What's his chances?"

The paramedic solemnly shook his head. "Hey, Jimmy. Get the suction," he shouted to the other paramedic coming with the cot.

The officer turned back to JD. "It's not looking good. What happened?"

"I hit him," JD answered.

"Excuse me?" the officer said.

"Something fell from his truck and hit my car. He refused to pay for the damage, so I punched him in the face. He fell and hit his head on a rock."

"You're admitting you might have killed this guy?"

JD shrugged. "I guess so," he answered. For some reason, he didn't care.

The officer spoke into his radio and then got out a pair of handcuffs. "Turn around."

JD put his hands on his trunk. It didn't seem fair. It wasn't JD's fault that the guy had damaged his new car. While the officer patted him down, the medics loaded the man into their truck. They were still doing CPR.

"Why am *I* under arrest?" JD asked. "Doesn't it

matter that *he* started this whole thing? Go look at the dent he put in my brand new car."

"That's all you're worried about? You know he's probably going to die because of you."

"This never would have happened if he wasn't so careless," JD snapped back. "Seriously, look at the way his truck is loaded. Isn't that against the law? I'm telling you, it's all his fault."

The officer cocked his head and then shook it. "I don't know, buddy. That's for the lawyers to fight out. For now, I'm taking you in." He escorted JD to the police cruiser and protected his head while guiding him onto the back seat. "My supervisor is on his way. Just sit tight for a bit."

JD swung his legs in and the officer closed the door. He looked out the window. Freddy stood by the old man's truck staring back. He lowered his head and shook it.

JD smirked. He wasn't as upset about his car anymore.

4
NOW

The first thing Daniel said to Maddy when he got home from work was to ask if she'd seen Jerry's comment. She shrugged her shoulders. "Some people are just jerks," she said.

Daniel couldn't understand how she could take such an insult in stride. It sat with him while he cleaned out the garage before dinner. He asked Maddy about it again at the table.

She answered, "Will you forget about that guy? It doesn't mean anything."

"Has he said anything else?"

"No."

Daniel stuffed a meatball into his mouth and chewed as Jerry's comment churned in his mind.

Already forgetting Jerry, Maddy announced, "I sold twenty mugs today."

Daniel's eyes widened. "Oh yeah. That reminds me." He dug in his pocket and pulled out Charlie's ten. "Make that twenty-one. Charlie wants a motto mug."

Maddy snatched the ten from his hand, never one to turn down cash. She did a cute little dance in her seat. She was so innocent and perfect. How could someone be so mean to her?

Your art is shit, Bitch.

His blood boiled as he chewed and faked a smile.

He listened to her talk about her day while he ate, but he didn't hear any more of what she said. Those social media tough guys were the worst. He had hated them when he had a CatchTime account, and he still did. It didn't seem fair that someone could say something so hurtful without any consequences. He felt his breaths quicken as he gazed at his plate.

"So, what's the plan tonight?" Maddy asked. When he didn't answer, she cleared her throat.

Daniel shook away his daze. "What?"

"I said, what do you want to do tonight?"

"I've gotta mow the yard."

She tilted her head. "Honey, you seem off. Is everything all right?"

Everything except what Jerry said, he thought. "Yeah. Everything's fine." He took their plates to the sink and washed them. As he scrubbed the dinner pans, he tried to imagine why Jerry would say something so harsh. He came up with nothing.

Your art is shit, Bitch.

Maddy got on tiptoe behind him and leaned around to kiss his cheek before heading to her she-shed to work on Charlie's mug.

Daniel went to the garage and gassed up his zero-turn mower. While he mowed the back yard, Jerry's comment ran through his mind over and over and made him angrier with each second that passed.

It was almost like he'd never cancelled his CatchTime account in the first place. All those angry, obsessive feelings were as raw today as they had been back then.

Your art is shit, Bitch.

Is it, Jerry? Is it really?

As he rode, he squeezed the handles so hard that his fingers went numb. After a few rows, he realized he had gotten off course and looked back at the curvy mow line behind him. After he finished his half-acre yard, he hardly remembered mowing at all.

Your art is shit, Bitch.

After weed-whacking and cleaning up the mower, Daniel took a shower. He stood under the water until the hot water ran out.

Your art is shit, Bitch.

Daniel shut off the water, dried off, and climbed into bed. He lay awake, staring at the ceiling for most of the night. Maddy climbed into bed around midnight, kissed his forehead and said goodnight, and then rolled over. Daniel's last thought before finally falling asleep was of Jerry. And his first thought when he woke up was of Jerry again.

Your art is shit, Bitch.

Maddy was already up and making breakfast. An egg sandwich and some bacon waited on the table. "Good morning," she said with a kiss on his cheek.

Daniel grunted.

"Are you still grouchy?" she asked.

"I just don't understand how you could blow off that comment."

"What comment?"

"You know. From Jerry?"

"Who's Jerry?"

"That guy. The one who … oh, never mind." Daniel finished his sandwich in quiet contemplation. He opened his phone where Jerry's comment was still on the screen. He glared at it, his anger growing again. He wondered who Jerry actually was and figured it couldn't hurt to take a look. After all, everything about Jerry was a simple touch of his name away. His finger hovered millimeters from the screen.

He took a deep breath in through his nose and let it out slowly from his mouth. He did it a second time, knowing further investigation would only drive him more bonkers. He set the phone on the table, proud of his restraint. He already felt better. He smiled at Maddy when she looked up from the book she was reading. She was beautiful.

Your art is shit, Bitch.

He ripped the phone from the table and touched Jerry's name. The first picture that popped up was of a young man in military fatigues. He had cropped hair and a mustache hiding part of a cocky smirk. He looked to be in his mid-twenties. Daniel scrolled down to the "about" section.

Full name: Jerry Davis

Favorite movie: Saving Private Ryan

Favorite food: MRE (Whatever that meant.)

Daniel scrolled a bit more.

Marriage status: Single and ready to mingle

Occupation: Freight Handler at Walmart

Daniel's first thought was to fire off a letter to Walmart and tell them the kind of things their employees were doing on social media. But that thought quickly faded with the realization of how petty he was being. As he continued to scroll, he came across something interesting.

Location: Newark, Ohio

"Well, I'll be," Daniel mumbled.

"What's that, honey?" Maddy asked, looking up from her book again.

Daniel stuffed his phone in his pocket. "Nothing. I was just surfing." But it wasn't nothing. It meant Jerry lived less than a half-hour away and Daniel could go visit him. If that was something he wanted to do, that is. Daniel got his phone back out and pulled up the premarket stocks. Ford looked to be up again. For the first time in a while, he didn't care.

Your art is shit, Bitch.

He gritted his teeth.

Daniel moved through the workday like a robot, his thoughts never far from Jerry. It wasn't fair that someone could enter his life, spew hateful things that might get a fella punched in a bar, and then vanish with no consequences.

Your art is shit, Bitch.

Charlie entered the breakroom and said, "Hi."

Daniel barely acknowledged him while mindlessly snacking on a bag of chips with his eyes locked on the table.

Charlie left with his can of soda.

It was obvious what needed to be done. If he didn't at least meet Jerry and ask him how he could be so mean to a complete stranger, he would obsess over it for weeks—if not months—and it would drive him mad. He never should have bought Maddy that ad space. He'd been doing so well staying away from social media. He decided driving to Walmart after work was his only choice to keep his sanity. Making a decision made him feel better immediately. He only hoped Jerry was working that night. His hands trembled with excitement. He looked around to make sure no one could see.

After his shift, he called Maddy as he crossed the parking lot to his car.

"What's up, babe?" she answered.

"I'm going to be a little late tonight. I need to run to Newark for an HDMI cable for the new TV."

"Why Newark? There's nowhere closer?"

"Nah. Everyone's out of what I need. But the Walmart website says there's one in stock in Newark."

"Okay. I'll put your dinner in the fridge."

Daniel climbed into his car. Before he started it, he rested his hands on the steering wheel. He told himself one last time to just let Jerry's comment slide.

Your art is shit, bitch.

He turned the ignition.

Even the half-hour drive to Newark didn't dampen his desire to meet Jerry. It might not be the right thing to do, but it was the right thing for *him*. He knew himself too well. He sat in his car in the Walmart parking lot and let the anger build just enough to push him forward.

An old man in a blue Walmart vest greeted him with a smile inside the store. "Good evening, sir," he said.

Daniel nodded and smiled back. He stopped next to the registers and scanned the aisles. He wasn't even sure he remembered what Jerry looked like from the one picture he'd seen. He saw an endcap display of HDMI cables and grabbed the right one, making a mental note to dispose of the one at home. Then he meandered toward the cash registers, his eyes still peeled.

A half-dozen people in blue Walmart aprons walked by. As they passed, he scanned their nametags for a Jerry. Or maybe Gerald. No luck.

This is stupid, he thought as he approached the registers. He pictured Maddy and sighed. Maybe he should strive to be more like her. Maybe not seeing Jerry was for the best. Maybe ...

He walked up to the self-checkout and swiped the

cable across the scanner.

"Leaving, Jerry?" the old man at the door asked.

Daniel spun toward him.

The guy from the CatchTime photo answered, "Just going for a smoke, Willard."

Daniel watched Jerry—that dirty bastard—pass through the doors with a ridiculous arrogance in his strut.

Your art is shit, Bitch.

To hell with Maddy's way. Daniel paid with cash, grabbed his receipt and the cable, and hurried through the doors as casually as he could. Once outside, he tucked the HDMI cable into his waistband and looked around the parking lot.

Jerry was pulling out a pack of cigarettes as he walked around the corner of the building toward the loading docks. Daniel looked around once more and then quietly followed.

Jerry's cigarette was short and skinny and smelled like pot, which explained why he would come out here instead of the designated employee smoking area. The loading docks faced a small, wooded area. It was dark with the lights near the bay doors providing the only illumination. Daniel quickened his pace to close the distance, his head on a swivel. There was no one around.

Once out of view of the front of the store, Daniel shouted, "Hey, Jerry."

Jerry flinched and spun around. "You're not supposed to be back here, dude." He gave Daniel a crooked look. "Do I know you?" He had the same cocky smirk as his profile picture.

Daniel stopped face to face with him. "Do you use CatchTime?"

Jerry's brow wrinkled. "Some. Why?"

"I got a question for you."

"I don't got much time left on my break." He took a hit of his joint.

Daniel made a fist at his side. "The other day you told someone online that her art wasn't very good. In fact, your exact words were 'Your art is shit, Bitch.'"

Jerry snorted, and smoke coughed from his nose. "Yeah, that was funny, huh?"

"No. No, it wasn't."

"What? Do you know her or something?"

"She's my wife."

"Okaaaay. So what?"

"I just wondered why you did it."

"I don't know, man. I don't like stupid birds, I guess. Chill out. Jeesh."

Daniel took a deep breath through his nose. He wanted to smash the jackass so bad. He bit his lip and held back. "Is that any way for a military guy to talk on social media?"

Jerry snorted again. "Military guy?"

"Yeah. Your profile pic shows you in fatigues and all your likes have to do with the military."

"Dude, are you CatchTime stalking me? That's creepy. Go find yourself some other hot guy to stalk. I'm not interested."

"You're not in the military?"

"Heck no. I'm just a fan."

"So, are you going to apologize?" Maybe a sincere apology could save Jerry a bunch of pain.

Jerry nodded. "Yeah, man. You win."

Daniel relaxed his shoulders.

Jerry smiled. "Tell that bitch I'm sorry her art is shit."

Daniel laid him out with a right hook before he could even fully process what Jerry had said. Jerry hit the ground hard. Daniel drew in a quivering breath and closed his eyes. It was happening again.

5
THEN

JD sat in the halfway house, his first few days of freedom really solidifying his desire to start a new life. Seven years in the joint for manslaughter was nothing to sneeze at.

First on his list for starting over was getting a job. A search of the community computer found two immediate possibilities for a guy with a record. One was for a job at Walmart, and the other was for a maintenance position. Since he wasn't keen on working retail, he decided to try the maintenance position first. He hoped a construction job would become available at some point, but in the meantime he would take what he could get. He just hoped he could get something better than Walmart.

The bus dropped him off two blocks south of the address in the downtown area. As he got closer to where he was headed, he realized it was a high-rise office building.

He straightened his shirt, tucking it in for the third time, took a deep breath, and then entered the lobby through the revolving door. The lobby was huge and immaculate. Escalators carried people to an eating area on the open second floor and elevators lined both side walls. A tree in a pot stood beside the door.

To his right was a security guard beside a metal detector. "This way, sir," the guard said.

JD emptied his pockets into the tray—two quarters, a key to the halfway house, and a wad of lint—passed through, and then collected his stuff. He searched for someone who might be able to give him an application.

There was an information desk on the opposite wall. He marched to it. The lady behind the desk had a brilliant smile that revealed two dimples. JD had a thing for dimples.

"How can I help you?" she asked. Her voice was bubbly and inviting.

"I'm … uh … looking for an application for a maintenance position."

"Oh, awesome." She pointed to a bank of computers with three other men tapping at the keyboards. "Good luck."

JD started to turn away as the lady lifted a coffee mug to her lips. She wasn't wearing a ring. He caught a glimpse of a little yellow bird on the mug. "What's on your mug?" he asked.

She pulled it away from her lips and held it out for him to see. "Just something I made. You like it?"

He reached out. "May I?"

"Sure."

He took the mug and examined it, careful not to spill her coffee. The bird was making a sculpture out of its nest. "Did you draw this?"

She bobbed her head. "Um-hm."

"It's great."

"Thank you."

"You should do art for a living."

She blushed. "You mean be a fulltime artist?"

"Sure."

"Well, my friend, paying the rent as an artist isn't exactly easy-peasy."

"Yeah, I don't imagine it is. Can I ask your name?"

"Madison. My friends call me Maddy."

JD held out his hand. "It's nice to meet you, Madison. I'm J—I mean, my name's Daniel."

Her face twisted slightly.

JD chuckled. "I'm sorry. My first name's James, but I go by my middle name now."

"Oh. Nice to meet you, Daniel." She shook his hand. "I hope you get the job."

"Me too."

He started to walk away, but hesitated. If he didn't say something now, he may never get the chance. He turned back. Madison was writing something. She looked up. "Is there something else?

He bashfully looked to the floor. "You know, I wouldn't be able to live with myself if I didn't ask you something."

"Oh?" She lowered her pen to the desk.

"Could we … I mean … Would you … uh … like to get some coffee sometime?"

Her lips curled upward slightly. "I don't know. Maybe."

"Great. Could I get your number?"

"Are you on CatchTime?" she asked as she wrote her number on a sticky note.

What the hell is CatchTime? he thought. He nodded anyway.

She scribbled something else on the sticky note. "This is my CatchTime ID. Request me as a pal and we can talk on there."

Daniel took her paper and nodded. As he walked away, he glanced over his shoulder. She smiled. He told himself, *I'm going to marry that girl one day . . . Well, after I figure out how to get on this CatchTime.*

6
NOW

Daniel stood over Jerry with adrenaline surging through his veins. He loved the feeling of power it gave him. It felt a little like when he'd killed the old man who damaged his Camaro, though not as potent. He'd love to get that feeling back again. He had relived it a thousand times over his seven years in prison.

He scanned the loading docks for witnesses. There was no one around. The lone security camera on the corner of the building pointed toward the bay doors and not toward the darkened area where Jerry and Daniel were.

Jerry looked up with wide, terrified eyes and a bloody lip. Daniel straddled his chest and delivered a solid blow to Jerry's face. Jerry wailed for help, so Daniel struck him again. "Shut up."

Amazingly, Jerry shut up.

Daniel was in ecstasy. He growled, "Give me your license."

"Wh-wh-what?" Jerry whimpered.

"Your license, asshole. Give it to me." He lifted his weight off Jerry just enough for Jerry to reach his rear pocket with a trembling hand. He shoved his wallet at Daniel's chest. "Take it, man. It's all yours."

Daniel wrapped his fingers in his shirt and took the wallet. Careful not to leave any fingerprints, he rifled through it and snatched Jerry's driver's license. Then he tossed the wallet aside, leaving a fifty-dollar bill half hanging out.

"Are you gonna let me go now?"

Daniel's expression turned dark. He shook his head. "No matter how many times I tell people not to fuck with people online, there's always some other wiseass who thinks he can get away with it."

Jerry's eyes danced nervously. Daniel grabbed a rock from the gravelly ground and lifted it above his head.

Jerry cried out and tried to squirm away. His shriek cut off abruptly as Daniel drove the rock against his temple. Jerry's body went limp. Daniel bashed his head three more times before he stopped.

Jerry's breaths came slow and sporadic.

Daniel watched the life leave Jerry's dull eyes. He sucked in a calming breath through his nose and then let it out through clenched teeth. He stood up and looked around again. It was still clear.

The weight of Jerry's hateful comment lifted from his soul and he sighed in relief. For the first time in days, he relaxed and his mind stopped twirling. He wondered why he had even debated coming at all. As Jerry lay dead at his feet, he had no doubt he had made the right decision. He would sleep like a hibernating bear when he got home.

He shoved the bloody rock into his coat pocket. Then he took one last look at Jerry's lifeless body, smiled, and walked to his car in the front parking lot. To anyone looking, he was just another shopper leaving the store.

On his way home, he pulled off the road and tossed the rock into a creek that ran under an overpass. Once he arrived home, he stopped in the laundry room and sprayed some stain remover on his coat and shirt before throwing them in the washer. Then he washed his hands and slung a clean T-shirt over his head.

Maddy shouted down from her she-shed, "Is that you, JD?" She was the only one he let call him that besides his mom.

"Yeah," he shouted back.

"There's chicken and a baked potato in the fridge."

"Okay. Thanks." Daniel went to his bedroom and pulled a safe out from under the bed. Careful to listen in case Maddy came down the hall, he spun the combination and opened the small safe. Inside was a 9MM pistol that his dad had given him before he died, some rare baseball cards worth a few thousand dollars, and a small wad wrapped in a handkerchief and a rubber band. He removed the rubber band and unwrapped the handkerchief. He whispered, "When are people going to learn how to act online?" Then he pulled Jerry's license from his back pocket and set it on the stack with nearly a dozen others.

With Jerry's license safely tucked away in his collection, he replaced the locked safe under the bed. Then he went to Maddy's she-shed where she sat in front of her computer. He put his hand on her shoulder and kissed her cheek. She leaned into his hand.

"Did you get what you needed in Newark?"

He grinned. "Oh yeah."

"Good."

"I'm going to go eat. I'm starvin'."

"Okay. I'll be down in a little bit."

He kissed her cheek again and she sighed in contentment. He couldn't have been happier.

END

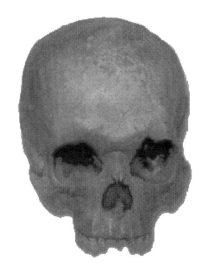

SKELWALLER LANE

"I cannot think of any need in childhood as strong as the need for a father's protection." ~ Sigmund Freud

I

Sweat poured from Billy's forehead. He'd never realized before how fast or how far he could run, but then he had never been chased by someone wanting to kill him, either. His face stung with the memory of fists pounding it. His nose bled like a waterfall regardless of how hard he pinched his nostrils shut. Some of the blood drained down the back of his throat, gagging him, yet he didn't slow.

He glanced at his button-down dress shirt which was now more red than white and plastered to his skin. His pursuer was relentless and Billy had barely escaped the beating.

The crescent moon in the sky wasn't giving off enough light for him to see very far ahead. Thank god he knew the country backroad as well as he did, otherwise he wouldn't have a chance. He glanced back. The bouncing beam of a flashlight still trailed him and seemed to be gaining ground. He panicked. He knew he could never stop, no matter how much his body begged him to rest. His pursuer seemed possessed. So Billy kept running, praying for a car to happen down the gravel lane. He knew his prayer wasn't likely to be answered. Few people traveled that lane because most knew about the house at the end. Billy's only hope was the interstate and the mom-and-pop gas station two miles ahead.

He hoped his lungs wouldn't give out before he made it, or that the bastard chasing him wouldn't get a second wind. Though he tried desperately to push himself beyond exhaustion, a sudden stitch in his side doubled him over. As he braced his hands on his knees and gasped for breath, he silently cursed his years of smoking. Deep breaths of manure-scented air didn't help. The dancing flashlight closed in. Billy could hear his pursuer's grunts as he ran.

Billy wheezed in another nasty lungful of air before he started running again. Even as he ran for his life, he couldn't shake the sick realization that the guy chasing him was as crazy as he was deadly.

Despite the pain, Billy kept running. Stopping surely meant death. The stranger's determined eyes had told him as much.

But Billy was too winded with too far to go. He needed rest, and he needed it soon. He was getting as close to his out-of-shape heart kicking his ass as the guy was to catching him.

There was a rusty, broken-down tractor beside the road up ahead. If he could get to it, maybe he could hide and the bastard would keep running. He just had to push himself until he got to it.

He was ready to surrender when he saw a glimmer of moonlight glint off the top of the tractor cab. Maybe it wasn't the salvation he'd convinced himself it would be, but the hope it represented gave him an extra little push. He almost collapsed in the ditch beside the tractor. He scurried through the overgrown weeds until he was beneath the green behemoth. John Deere had just become his best friend. Motionless, he watched the road.

The stranger's flashlight slowed and stopped. Billy tried to hold his breath so the stranger wouldn't hear him, but that only made his next gasp louder. *Keep going,* he silently begged.

He lay on his back like a rock in the high grass, terrified his heart's frenetic beats would alert the bastard as it tried to burst through his sternum.

The flashlight beam scanned the field before resting on the tractor. "I know you're down there," the man shouted, his voice deep and angry. Billy tensed. Hearing that merciless voice again turned his stomach. At least he was catching his breath.

Unfortunately, his attacker was as well. The man cautiously climbed down into the ditch.

Billy slowly felt along the ground until his fingers touched a rock the size of his fist. He quietly and methodically dug away the packed dirt around it until he could pull it free.

The sound of rustling grass continued until it stopped several feet from the back end of the tractor. Billy was closer to the front. He couldn't move, fear planting him to the ground. From his angle, he couldn't see the man. He wanted to cry. Dying in a lonely field with his body possibly never being found was too awful to contemplate.

Out of the corner of his eye, he saw the flashlight beam scan the grass beside him. Billy didn't move. The silence was murder. How long could he just lay there waiting to die? He slowly turned his head. The flashlight beam crossed the grass again and stopped on his face. He swallowed hard.

The air dripped with coming violence. Billy's face couldn't withstand another punch. It already felt swollen and deformed. He was pretty sure his nose was broken.

The man snarled, "Get out here, you bastard." He lunged, slowed by the thick grass.

Billy scrambled farther under the tractor.

"I'll kill you," the man shouted. His outstretched

hand caught Billy's ankle. Billy shrieked. With the luckiest kick ever, Billy freed his foot. He scurried to the other side closest to the road. Before he could get out of the ditch, a thick, powerful hand grabbed his bloody shirt from behind.

"Please don't hurt me anymore," he begged.

The man grabbed his throat, shined the flashlight beam in his eyes, and screamed, "Where is—"

Billy swung the rock with all his might. The man grunted when it slammed into his temple. Blood splattered across Billy's face. For once it wasn't his. The man tumbled backward into the weeds, his flashlight flopping from his hand. Billy should have stayed and finished him off, but he was too scared and too focused on escaping. He climbed back onto the road and staggered toward the interstate.

Seeing the lights of the store ahead gave his legs renewed strength. He prayed someone would be there.

As he got closer, he saw an old, beat-up pickup truck in the gravel parking lot. The mismatched red door on the primer-grey body told him it was the owner's. He might have smiled if his face didn't hurt so bad. He glanced back, hoping his tormenter hadn't yet recovered, but to his dread he saw the flashlight bobbing along the road again. Knowing how hard he had struck the man made him wonder if it was the Terminator chasing him. Billy kept running.

The lighted marquee sign was supposed to read "Frank's Gas," but the "F" had burned out years ago, leaving only "rank's gas." He ran past the pickup truck and burst through the front door. The bell jingled above it.

An elderly lady sat with her chin propped up by her hands and her eyes closed.

"Help," he screamed.

She jolted awake, grabbed her chest, and backed away from the counter. "What are you doing?" she cried. One look at his face made her gasp. "What happened to you?"

"You gotta help me. Do you have a gun?"

"Heavens, no."

"Do you have anything to protect us?"

She looked behind the counter and reluctantly lifted a baseball bat. She didn't hand it over. "What's the matter?"

"There's a man trying to kill me."

She covered her mouth with her free hand. "Oh, lordy. Now, slow down. Why is someone trying to kill you?"

Billy lunged across the counter, startling her. He yanked the bat from her hand. "You've got to lock the doors. Fast."

She grabbed a keyring from behind the counter. "Now, wait just a minute. Should I call the p—"

"No time," Billy snapped and turned back to the entrance just as the bells above the door jingled again.

Billy nearly pissed his pants. The stranger almost filled the doorway with his girth. A trail of gore ran down the side of his face from his temple. He casually swiped at it as though the blood was inconsequential. More blood—Billy's blood—stained his hands. He breathed in deep, angry breaths.

Billy whispered to the lady behind the counter, "Give me the keys to your truck." He didn't look at her, but heard the keys rattle in her shaky hand. She set them in his outstretched palm. With his other hand, he raised the bat above his head. "I don't want to hurt you, mister," he said.

The man sneered. His eyes filled with rage. He

charged, closing the gap in a fury. Billy swung the bat, but the man tackled him before it could connect.

What little breath Billy had recovered exploded from his lungs as he hit the floor. The man landed on top of him, straddling his chest. He drove his thick fist at Billy's left eye and the world briefly turned white.

"Where is she?" the man shouted.

"I don't know," Billy cried. "Who?"

"Bullshit." He punched Billy again.

The old lady screamed for help, too terrified to come out from behind the counter. Billy hoped to god someone with a gun was in the back.

The man ignored her.

Billy tried to shake the fuzz away, but the man hit him again.

"Tell me," the man shouted. He bounced to his feet and grabbed Billy's shirt collar and twisted the fabric tight around Billy's neck. Billy fought his powerful grip as the man dragged him, kicking, toward the counter and snatched a hunting knife from a sales display.

"Oh my god," the lady cried, and backed up against the cigarettes.

The man used his teeth to tear open the packaging. He held the eight-inch blade in his free hand and knelt over Billy, pressing his back against the cold floor.

Billy begged, "Please, don't kill me. I didn't do anything."

The man touched the blade to Billy's left side below his ribs. "Last chance," he growled.

"I-I-I don't know what you're talking about."

The man slowly shoved the blade into Billy's flesh. Billy cried out.

The man was a demon.

"Stopstopstopstop," Billy shrieked as the blade sank deeper and deeper. His eyes went wide and he gasped.

The man paused, the knife halfway in Billy's chest.

"Please. No more. Just kill me if that's what you're going to do. I don't want to hurt anymore."

"I don't want you dead, you fucker. Not yet." He slowly withdrew the knife, allowing the serrated edge to rip through Billy's flesh again. Removing the knife opened the floodgates. Blood poured onto the cream-colored linoleum floor and puddled around them. The old lady screamed like she was the one being skewered.

The man grabbed Billy's collar again and pulled his face close. "You tell me what I need to know or it'll get worse."

"I swear I don't know what you're talking about," Billy cried again.

The man grabbed Billy's wrist and severed his pinky finger with one swipe. Billy grimaced, and then the pain truly took hold. He buried his face against the man's leg and screamed. The pain shooting up his arm was like a wave of fire. "Please," he cried.

"It ain't over yet, you bastard. Where is she?"

Billy sobbed, unable to gather himself enough to answer. He tried to fight back, but the man punched him again, causing his body to go momentarily limp. The man ripped open Billy's shirt.

"You've done enough," Billy cried. "Leave me alone." The hate on the man's face told Billy that his pleas were useless. Without remorse, the man dug the point of the knife into Billy's chest in short, bloody strokes. When he finished, he stood up.

As the blood openly flowed from Billy's side, he felt the world dimming. The pain from his missing finger went numb. He choked back vomit or blood, he wasn't sure. The man patiently watched while Billy's world faded. The old lady's screams blurred into the background.

Billy strained to look down at his own bloody chest. He was dying, there was no doubt. And with the life oozing from his body, his eyes focused on the single word carved into his chest. Even upside down, he could read it.

PEDOPHILE

2
TWO HOURS EARLIER

Thomas rotated the basketball in his hands as the carnival booth attendant explained how to win a humongous teddy bear for his five-year-old daughter. All he had to do was make three baskets in ten tries. He knew the basketball rim was likely the same size as the ball itself, but if anyone could do it, it was him. You didn't get to be his size without someone convincing you to play basketball at some point in your life.

It was crowded, so he pulled Chloe close to his leg. "Stay here, sweetie."

She nodded and pulled a piece of cotton candy off the stick with her teeth.

After ten tosses, Thomas hadn't made a single shot.

The carny leaned in with a consolation rubber lizard. "You did your best, buddy." There was a little snark in his tone.

"Yeah. Thanks." Thomas took the lizard and turned to Chloe. He started to apologize for not winning the bear, but stopped cold. She wasn't standing next to him anymore. "Chloe?" he called. He scanned the crowd. "Chloe?"

A line was building behind him and the carny motioned for him to get out of the way. "Hey, buddy. Could you move aside?" he said.

Thomas glanced back, confusion and panic setting

in. "What?"

The carny motioned him aside again and mouthed, "Move it."

Thomas stepped out of the line and looked around the side of the booth. "Chloe?" he shouted, increasingly frantic. His heart dropped into his gut. She knew better than to wonder off. He grabbed a stranger's arm.

She recoiled.

"I'm sorry," he said. "Did you see the five-year-old little girl who was standing right here?"

The lady shook her head. Thomas grabbed the next person and she too denied seeing any little girls. He felt panic rise from his gut and tried unsuccessfully to calm himself. A group of teenagers stood with their bikes next to the lemon shake stand and he ran to them. They hadn't seen her either.

He couldn't believe she would walk away. She was so good—she would never leave his side. "Chloe," he shouted, his voice quivering. "Chloe."

People started to stare, but he didn't care.

As he scanned the crowd, he saw a commotion near the entrance gates and leaned around someone for a better view. A man pushed people out of his way while carrying something toward the parking lot. Thomas pushed closer. No, not something. Someone. *Oh my god. Chloe.*

"Hey," Thomas screamed, and pushed into the crowded main drag toward the gates. "Stop him. Stop that man," he shouted. The people surrounding him stopped and stared, confused. The man carrying Chloe slipped through the gate and ran into the parking lot.

No, no. Please, no. "Someone help me," Thomas shouted again. As he plowed his way through the gates, a young man wearing a yellow staff jacket intercepted him. "What is it, sir?" the man asked.

Thomas shoved the man aside. He was panicked, screaming relentlessly for Chloe. More people gathered as he scanned the parking lot.

A woman in the crowd approached. "Is everything all right?"

"My daughter …," he whispered, barely loud enough for her to hear. "Someone took my daughter."

She lifted her hand to her mouth. "Oh my."

Thomas pressed his hands to his temples. His world was crumbling and he couldn't do anything to stop it.

"Did you call the police?" the woman asked.

The police. On the verge of tears, he said, "Find a phone. Call the police. My daughter's name is Chloe Baker. She's five. I'm Tom Baker." He could barely get out the words.

She nodded and started jogging toward a bank of payphones near the entrance of the carnival.

A car engine revved with a rattle like the muffler was barely hanging on. A late '70s model black Honda Civic hatchback raced toward the exit. The driver's door sported a large dent.

Tom shouted to the lady headed for the payphones, "Tell them he's in a black Civic hatchback with a dented door. I can't see the plates."

The Civic nearly plowed into a parking attendant who had to dive out of the way to avoid being hit. Thomas sprinted after the car as it sped away. He collapsed to his knees beside the attendant.

The kid stood up and dusted himself off. He shoved out his middle finger and shouted, "Slow down, Billy, you asshole."

Thomas jerked his head around. "What did you

say?"

The attendant looked at him like he'd asked the square root of a million. "I called him an asshole."

"No. Before that."

"I told Billy to slow down."

Thomas grabbed his shirt. "You know that man in the Civic?"

The kid pulled away. "Hey, man, don't touch me."

"I'm sorry. Please, just answer me. Do you know that guy?"

"I don't *know* him. I know who he is, if that's what you mean. He comes here every year and talks to the kids as they come in. Sometimes he dresses like a cartoon character. If you ask me, I think he's a creep."

Oh my god. "What's his name?"

"Billy. I already told you that."

"No, his whole name."

"I'm not sure. Hurd … Holder … something like that. Why do you want to know?"

"He just drove away with my little girl. Do you know where he lives?"

"Not really."

"Think. Please, think."

"I heard he lives somewhere on Skelwaller Lane, but I wouldn't know for sure. I've never been there."

Thomas sprinted across the parking lot to his car, fumbling for his keys on the way. He knew Skelwaller Lane crossed under Interstate 70, but that was about it. His car rumbled to life. He jammed the gearshift into drive and floored it, sending dirt and gravel flying at the other cars in the lot. He shot passed the kid at the entrance. The kid shouted something at him, probably calling him an asshole too.

He gunned the engine toward the interstate. The lines of the road blurred behind tears as he imagined all the horrible things that could happen or could already be happening. His speedometer hit 90 MPH and he prayed for the flashing lights of a Highway Patrol cruiser to appear in his rearview mirror.

None did.

3

The interstate didn't have an exit to Skelwaller Lane, so Thomas had to get off at the exit before it. He flew along the side streets until he reached a T-junction where a mom-and-pop filling station sat. Left appeared to lead to several neighborhoods while right led down a dark, narrow dirt road. He had a choice to make. He turned onto the dirt road. God, he hoped he was right.

With no streetlights or houses along the road, the only sign of life was an old, broken-down tractor next to a ditch. Thomas drove nearly a mile, terrifying doubts eating at his insides. Maybe he should turn back. There was no reason Billy couldn't live in a regular neighborhood. And if he had a garage, Thomas would never find him.

He was looking for somewhere to make a U-turn when the crescent moon highlighted the outline of a dark house in the distance. Thomas slowed to a stop. That had to be it. What better place to hide for someone who kidnapped little girls? If nothing else, he could turn around there. He crept forward slowly so as to not alert anyone who might be there. Surprise was his best bet. He turned off his headlights.

Before he reached the house, a set of taillights in the gravel driveway brightened. An engine roared to a start with the same rattling muffler as the Civic. Thomas stopped. The Civic's reverse lights lit up and it slowly backed down the driveway toward

Skelwaller Lane.

Thomas pulled off the side of the road and put his car in park so the red glow of his brake lights wouldn't give him away. Fury unlike any he had ever felt in his life rushed through him. He rubbed his thigh until his palm was nearly on fire from the friction against his blue jeans. As the Civic backed onto the lane and faced him, he took a deep breath. Thomas closed his eyes and said a small prayer. Then he jammed his car into drive and mashed the gas pedal. He flipped on his headlights, no longer concerned with stealth. The driver of the Civic didn't have time to react before Thomas was on him. Thomas braced himself for the impact.

Metal collided with metal with an ear-splitting din. Glass shattered and exploded through the air. Thomas's chest slammed the steering wheel and his head whipped forward before jerking violently back. He blinked repeatedly to clear his eyes.

The smashed Civic leaked smoke from beneath its crumpled hood. The driver's door creaked open, glass raining to the ground, and the driver dropped one foot to the road. He pulled himself out, wobbled, and caught himself by clutching his open door. His nose bled profusely onto his white button-down shirt. He appeared dazed, standing in the beam of Thomas's lone surviving headlight. He was the same man from the carnival, the one the kid at the parking entrance had called Billy.

Thomas wrenched his car door open, surprised he was able. This could be his last chance. He leaped from the car, be damned the pain in his throbbing shoulder and aching chest. His vision blurred. He'd heard of people seeing red with rage, but never believed it could be literal until now.

He ran to Billy, grabbed his shirt, and screamed, "Where's my daughter?"

Wobbly and dazed, Billy leaned his head against Thomas's chest. Thomas shoved him away and screamed again, "Where is she?" before punching the man's face.

Billy didn't answer, so Thomas held him up and hit him again. He would continue hitting Billy until Billy was dead if that's what he had to do.

When Billy looked like he'd had enough and was ready to talk, Thomas stopped hitting him long enough for him to point weakly at his hatchback. Thomas tossed him to the ground and raced to the rear hatch of the Civic. The window had black plastic duct-taped over it. Of course it was locked.

Thomas shot to the driver's door, reached in, and yanked the keys from the ignition. Inside the hatch was a blanket wrapped around something that didn't move.

Please, God. No.

He lifted the blanket, only to find dirty shovels and duct tape. His knees went weak and he almost fell. He couldn't let his mind go to why the bastard had shovels. "You son of a bitch," he shouted as he slammed the hatch shut.

He raced to the front where he'd left Billy lying on the ground, but the kidnapper wasn't there. Thomas looked around until he caught a glimpse of him running along the lane. Billy was smart; he knew if he had tried to run toward the house, he would have needed to pass Thomas and he never would have made it. Choosing the road gave him a nice head start.

Thomas ran to his own car, reached in the glovebox for a flashlight, and gave chase.

4
NOW

Billy lay bleeding on the linoleum floor at Thomas's feet. He looked down at the letters carved into his chest and smirked even as the lifeblood slowly oozed from the knife wound in his side.

Thomas bent over and grabbed Billy's hair. Billy started laughing.

"What are you laughing at?" Thomas snarled.

Billy gagged and choked, leaking blood from the corner of his mouth. He whispered something Thomas couldn't hear.

Thomas leaned closer. "What?" he growled.

"I said …" Blood splattered Thomas's cheek as Billy tried to speak. "… I said you'll never find her in time. My brother will be home soon. And when he gets there, he has plans for your little girl. In fact, he's probably there now."

Thomas felt a kick in the gut that nearly doubled him over. The blood drained from his face. He collapsed to his rear, the hunting knife dangling from loose fingers. He remembered the dirty shovels in Billy's trunk and realized they weren't there because they had already been used, but because they were about to be. His daughter was still in the house, and he had left her there. He rubbed his eyes with his bloody palm. He dry heaved.

As Billy lay bleeding on the cold floor, his

breathing slowed. Thomas stood up. With one last look at Billy, he saw him sigh his last breath.

Maybe Billy was right and his brother was already home. But maybe he was wrong. Thomas made a fist. He lifted his eyes to the terrified store owner. "Call the police," he said hoarsely.

"What?" she asked.

"Call the police," he shouted. "Tell them this bastard kidnapped my daughter and has her at his house at the end of Skelwaller Lane." He snatched the old lady's truck keys from Billy's limp fingers and raced through the door. Thanks to God, the junk heap of a truck actually started. He tore out of the lot and sped along the lane to where his totaled car and Billy's Civic blocked the road.

He jumped out and ran the rest of the way up the drive to the dark two-story house. The front porch leaned to one side and one of the gutters hung to the ground. He crept onto the porch and rattled the door handle. To his surprise, it was unlocked. With one fist clenched at his side, he pushed it open.

The foyer was empty. The walls were bare, peeling paint and yellow stains showing their wear. There wasn't a picture in sight. Thomas hesitated, listening for any signs of life. All he could hear was his own heart pounding in his chest. He held his breath.

And then he heard a faint noise from upstairs. His stomach turned. Though it was only a whimper, it gave him hope. He tore up the staircase. The hallway was dimly lit by a lamp with a naked bulb sitting on a small table at the opposite end. He heard a child sniffle and whimper again. It came from behind a door near the lamp. Thomas crept to the door and gently grabbed the handle. Then he turned it and swung the door open. He burst into the room.

Plastic covered the hardwood floor and black walls. There wasn't any furniture save a single floor lamp. It flickered like it had a loose wire. In the opposite corner a little girl stood facing the wall like she was being punished. Thomas choked back vomit.

"Chloe," he whispered. "Honey, are you okay?"

The few seconds that it took for her to answer stretched on for a lifetime. She finally nodded, though she still didn't turn away from the corner. She whispered, "He was going to give me candy."

Thomas ran to her and swept her into his arms. It felt like a miracle to hold his angel again. He squeezed her with all he had as his tears flowed. He pulled her away and looked into her brown eyes. "We have to leave, honey. You're all right, but you need to stay with me, okay?"

"Will you carry me, Daddy?" she asked. "I'm scared. The big man said he would be back soon."

He wanted to carry her more than anything, but he needed to be ready for Billy's brother. He whispered, "I will, honey. I just can't yet. We need to get out of here first."

"He said I was bad and I was in trouble. He said I couldn't leave this room."

"Don't listen to him, honey. You didn't do anything wrong. He did. He was the bad one."

Thomas led her toward the door, but sickening sounds from the stairwell stopped him cold.

Clomp.

Thump.

Clomp.

Thump.

Whoever was coming dragged something behind them. The sound of those thumps sent shivers up Thomas's spine.

He searched for a way out. Boards covered the only window. He pushed the plastic-covered door until only a crack was left open through which he could watch the stairwell. The top of a man's balding head rose beyond the open railing.

Thomas whispered, "Honey, get in the closet." He gently nudged her into the closet and crammed himself in behind her. He quietly pulled the door closed.

"Chloooeee?" the man called from the hallway. As he pushed the door open he said, "I have your candy, but we have to hurry because someone might be coming and we don't want them to know what you've done."

Thomas's blood boiled. Chloe squeezed his hand. She was being so brave, and he was proud of her. He squeezed her hand back. The footsteps and the horrible dragging sound that followed moved across the room toward them.

Thomas felt Chloe struggle in his grip and realized that he was squeezing too hard. He let go of her hand.

The footsteps stopped just outside the closet door. Chloe's breath stuttered from her quivering lips. Thomas's own breath was catching in his throat.

He gently brushed Chloe's cheek with his finger. Even in the darkness, he could feel her looking up at him. He had always been her hero and he'd be damned if that was going to change. He would fight the devil himself if it meant saving her. He made a fist.

The silence hurt his ears. He wondered if the man knew she was in there. He wondered if—

The head of a sledgehammer crashed through the door next to his face. Chloe shrieked. Thomas stumbled back and then steeled his resolve. He kicked the door open as the man drew back the sledgehammer again.

Stunned, the man reeled backward. He was shirtless and fat with his saggy gut hanging over his belt. His eyes went wide. Thomas pounced. The man surprised him with his speed and swung the hammer with all his might.

Thomas threw his arms in front of his face. He heard his left forearm snap long before he felt it. The momentum of the swing sent him to the floor while the man clumsily followed him down. Thomas winced, trying not to show how injured he was.

"Run, Chloe," he screamed.

The man rolled toward the closet as Chloe burst out and raced past his outstretched hands.

"Don't stop until someone helps you, baby," Thomas shouted as she charged through the open door.

The man tried to get up, but Thomas grabbed his waistband with his good arm. The man struck Thomas's jaw with the butt of the sledgehammer's handle. Thomas saw white. His grip faltered. The man chased Chloe into the hall. Thomas shook away the blow and gave chase, his shattered left arm hanging uselessly at his side.

Chloe shrieked near the top of the stairs. Thomas plowed through the doorway and stumbled against the table with the lamp. It fell to its side but didn't break. When he saw Chloe, he froze, his stomach in knots.

The man stood behind her at the top of the stairs with one sweaty hand across her chest and the other holding a knife. He trembled, seemingly more afraid of Thomas than Thomas was of him.

Thomas calmly righted himself and held his good hand out in front of his chest. His shattered arm throbbed with even the slightest movements.

"It's all good, buddy," he said, surprised at how calm he sounded. "I won't hurt you if you just let her go. Please."

At first the man stood quietly, a string of drool dangling from the corner of his lips. After an eternity, he whispered, "You really promise you won't hurt me?"

That was the last thing Thomas expected to hear, but it gave him a chance. Though he wanted to kill the man like he had Billy, he would give the devil himself a pass if it meant saving his daughter. "Oh god, yes. I promise. Please, just let her go."

"Where's my brother?"

Thomas had to think fast. Figuring the man must have seen Billy's wrecked Civic, he had to be careful with his answer. "I chased him, but he ran into the field and got away."

The man tilted his head and stared as if examining Thomas for lies. Thomas didn't waver. His daughter's life depended on him selling it.

"And that's your car that smashed Billy's?" the man asked.

"Yes. Yes, it's my car."

"If that's your car, then whose truck is beside it?"

Oh, shit.

Thomas bowed his head. He had forgotten about the truck. "Listen. I chased your brother, but he got away. I walked to the gas station at the end of the lane and borrowed their truck."

The man's eyes widened. "Did you call the police?"

Thomas shook his head. "I didn't, but the lady at the store might have. If you just let Chloe go, you can get away before they get here. Man, you can believe me when I say if you hurt her, I'm going to kill you in an incredibly painful way. This is your only chance to get away. Take it."

"Remember, you promised?"

"Yes. Yes. I promise. Go." Thomas cautiously took a step forward.

The man slowly lifted his arm from Chloe's chest and Thomas calmly waved her to him. She ran to him and clung to his leg.

Flashing lights flickered through the plastic room's window.

The man cautiously backed onto the steps. "You promised to let me go. Don't you dare welch."

Thomas breathed in deep through his nose. Then he nodded in reluctant agreement. The man turned and ran down the stairs, through the house, and out the back door.

Thomas fell to his knees. Chloe dove against his chest and he wrapped his good arm around her.

"Come on, honey. Let's get out of here."

He carried her down the stairs and through the front door where three police officers stood on the lawn with their guns drawn. He lowered Chloe to the ground, raised his uninjured arm in the air, and knelt on the porch. The cops swarmed him as a female officer scooped Chloe into her arms. Chloe screamed for her daddy and reached her arms out to him.

"He's getting away," Thomas said calmly.

"Keep it quiet," one of the officers barked. He grabbed Thomas's broken arm and Thomas winced. The officer said, "We saw what you did at Frank's."

Thomas was careful not to raise his voice. "I was only trying to find my daughter. If you just let me explain—"

"Yeah, well, the detectives will sort all that out."

"The real bad guy's getting away," he repeated.

More cruisers skidded in the gravel behind the stolen truck. The officer next to Thomas pointed toward the house and shouted, "Go around back. There's another suspect fleeing into the woods behind the house."

Thomas smiled, hopeful that the kidnapper wouldn't get away after all.

The officer gingerly helped Thomas to his feet and led him to a cruiser. "We'll get that arm looked at as soon as we can, sir. We just need to sort some of this out first."

Thomas sat in the back seat as ordered. He scanned the other cruisers until he locked eyes with Chloe. She sweetly waved.

He mouthed, "I love you." If he just saw her dimples, he'd know everything would be okay.

She smiled.

Nothing that happened next could hurt him now.

Before the officer closed the door, seven shots rang out from the forest behind the house.

Thomas lowered his head and smiled.

END

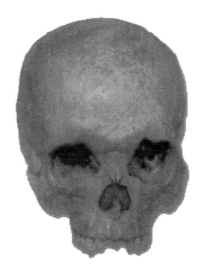

DOA

"Death is the great revealer of what is in a man, and in its solemn shadow appear the naked lineaments of the soul." ~ Edwin Hubbel Chapin

I

The lieutenant stood at the front of the engine bay for the start of a fresh twenty-four-hour shift. He held a clipboard and a pencil. The crew wandered to their positions as the overhead speaker announced it was time for roll call. Toni stood closest to the medic truck beside her partner for the day, Steve. She loved her job. And she liked working with Steve in particular because he was at the top of his game and never shy about sharing his knowledge. Rarely did a shift pass without him teaching her a veteran trick or two.

Toni barely listened to the lieutenant rattle off the assignments, though she did hear him say it was a holiday routine, which basically meant that once all the station duties were completed the afternoon belonged to the firefighters. She'd been looking forward to some downtime so she could catch up on a clever little novel she had been reading about werewolves as pets. After the lieutenant finished, Toni and Steve worked their way to the back doors of the medic truck.

"You wanna drive today?" she asked.

He climbed into the back without answering, which was odd because usually he was already two coffees in and gabbing away.

"Steve," she called.

He turned, surprised. "Oh, I'm sorry, Toni. Did you say something?"

"Yeah. I asked if you wanted to drive. Is

213

everything all right?"

"Sure. Everything's fine. I just had an argument with Helen this morning, that's all. So now, not only do I have to work on Christmas, I have to do it while not speaking to my wife. Well ... she's not speaking to me, if I'm being honest."

Toni followed him into the medic truck and sat on the bench seat. "I'm sorry to hear that. What'd you do wrong?" She grinned to let him know she was only tweaking him a bit.

He brushed her off with a wave and answered, "It's nothing. We argue all the time nowadays." He paused and looked down at his hands. It was the first time he had alluded to problems at home, and she felt bad for him.

Then he broke the awkward silence by slapping his hands together, startling her. His eyes lit up. "Hey, let's forget about all that and have a good day today."

That sounded good to Toni. She set the airway kit on the bench and opened it, checking the intubation tools. Trying to stick a tube down someone's throat in the midst of a life-or-death emergency wasn't the right time to find out that the last shift had used the exact size tube she needed and forgotten to replace it. Or that the bulb on the laryngoscope was dead. Everything was good in the intubation kit, but the oxygen bottle was low. She swapped the regulator from the low bottle to a fresh full one.

Steve reached past her and removed a nasal cannula from the airway kit. "Have you ever seen how to use one of these to flush out someone's eyes?"

She shook her head.

"Oh, cool. You'll like this. First, you have to have the patient lying on their back." He held up the two prongs that typically inserted into a person's nostrils and straddled them over the bridge of his own nose with the prongs pointing to the inside corner of each eye. "Now you just wedge the other end of the hose into some IV tubing, feed it into an IV bag, and let it flow into their eyes. It works great. Watch." He reached for an IV bag just as the truck's computer chimed with an emergency call.

The overhead PA crackled and the computerized voice of the dispatcher blared throughout the station. "Medic fourteen. Engine fourteen. Behind 1692 Smyth Road on a report of a possible DOA. CPD is responding." Toni closed the airway kit and put it back in the compartment. She climbed out of the back and into the front passenger seat while Steve hopped in the driver's seat.

"It's too early to be dealing with dead bodies," he said with a sigh.

Toni pressed the en route button and scanned the computer screen for any dispatcher notes.

"What's it say?" Steve asked as he shifted the truck into gear and waited for the overhead door to lift.

"Says a couple kids found a body behind their house on the bank of the river. It looks like he's been dead for a while."

Steve gave it some gas. "I'd say this isn't the best way to start our Christmas shift, huh?"

"No, I don't believe it is."

Toni slipped on her coat and a winter hat, her ponytail poking out the back. They approached Smyth Road. She pointed to two adults and two kids standing at the end of a driveway with a police officer. She saw their misty breaths in the cold. The kids appeared to be seven or eight at the most.

Toni climbed out and retrieved the airway kit just in case the person wasn't actually dead. Steve grabbed the medicine kit.

"What's up?" she asked as she approached the police officer. He was an older cop that had always come off as gruff and unfriendly on her previous dealings with him.

He barely looked up when he answered, "These two kids were having a snowball fight down by the river and came across a body. I was just getting ready to head down there."

"Okay. We'll walk with you."

Toni, Steve, and the police officer started around the house. They followed a trail of footsteps in the snow across the half-acre back yard and down a wooded hill to the river's edge.

While they were searching, the engine crew arrived at the top of the hill. "What do you need down there, Toni?" the lieutenant shouted.

"I don't know yet, Lieu. We haven't found anybody—" Just as she said it, her eyes fell on a tree sticking out of the water. Staring back from its base was the distorted, bloated, half-missing face of a man. He was hung up on the trunk and had probably been there for a while. His legs floated with the current and he wasn't wearing any pants under his dark-blue sweatshirt. Parts of his body were decayed black and blue.

"Welp. I guess I found him." She nodded toward the tree.

The officer and Steve turned. Steve keyed his radio and said, "Code One time," which meant the victim was indeed dead on arrival.

Toni shouted up to the lieutenant, "He's deader than a doornail, Lieu. We're good down here. We don't need anything." She turned back to the body as the engine crew returned to their truck. No matter how many dead bodies she had already seen in her short career, it was still a bit jarring. She tilted her head slightly. There was nothing quite like looking into the empty eyes of someone who had passed. It was like gazing into a doll's eyes with nothing behind them. It gave her the creeps, yet she found it difficult to turn away. As she watched his bloated corpse bob with the current, she started to wonder what circumstances could lead a guy to end up pantsless in a river.

She didn't realize she was staring until Steve nudged her arm. "You good?" he asked.

She shook herself. "Yeah. Of course. I'll go get the report pad and take these kits back to the truck."

Steve nodded.

Toni climbed the hill, replaced the kits in their compartment, and opened the passenger door to grab the report computer.

"Hi there," someone said from the driver's seat.

She jumped and nearly pissed her pants. "Who the fuck are you? And why are you in my truck?"

He smiled. He was missing a front tooth. "Relax," he said calmly. "I just wanna talk for a minute." He was a husky guy wearing grey sweatpants and a blue hooded sweatshirt. His dark hair was cropped close along the sides and touched the bottom of his neck in the back. He tapped the passenger seat. "Climb in. Talk to me for a second."

Toni didn't want to climb in. She cautiously lifted the walkie microphone to her mouth.

The stranger shook his head. "You don't need that," he said, and the light on her walkie went dead.

She squeezed it and nothing happened.

"I'm not going to hurt you," he said.

Her eyes met his. They were hollow and dead and

hypnotizing. She couldn't look away, and before she knew it she had climbed in and closed the door.

He smiled again. "That's better."

Her confidence drained from her every pore. "Wh-who are you?"

He scoffed. "You don't recognize me? We just met down by the river."

By the river? And then the significance of the blue sweatshirt hit her. "Oh." But this guy didn't look anything like the body she had just seen.

"I know what you're thinking," he said. "I've been down there for a while. Being dead does quite a number on someone's looks. You just wait until you see how *you* look three weeks after you die. Not to mention floating in a river and feeding the critters."

Stunned, Toni had to consciously retract her hanging jaw just to say, "I-I'm sorry."

The man blew her off with a wave.

Toni looked through the window toward the back of the house in hopes that either Steve, the police officer, or both were coming, but there was no one there. Then she noticed something strange. Nothing was moving. There were no cars, no people, nothing. She glanced toward the sky and saw an airplane frozen in mid-flight. "What's going on?" she asked, much calmer than she'd expect to be.

"I told you. I want to talk for a minute."

Toni pulled the door handle, but the door didn't open.

The stranger grumbled, "Let me know when you're ready to get started."

Toni turned back to him.

He sighed. "Good. Now, as we've already established, that's me down by the river. And I need your help."

"What happened to you?"

"I fell in somewhere upstream."

"How?"

"What do you mean, how? I got too close to the edge. I didn't want to fall in." He shook his head. "Are you going to keep asking dumb questions or can we get on with this?"

"I'm sorry."

"You keep saying that."

Toni bowed her head, afraid to ask anything else.

He shifted uncomfortably in his seat. "You're probably wondering why I wasn't wearing any pants."

She shrugged shyly.

"It's nothing weird or anything. The current pulled these stupid sweatpants off after I fell in." He pinched the fabric on his thigh and tugged it outward a bit. "And the water was pretty cold, so don't go judging me on anything you saw down there, either."

She shook her head.

He leaned over and swatted her shoulder. "Relax. I'm just kidding."

She nodded.

"You're not too fun, are you?"

"I'm just scared, sir."

"Why are *you* scared? I'm the one who's dead. I've got no idea what happens next."

She nodded again. "So, what do you want with me, sir?"

"First, I want you to see me as a person and not just some corpse you found down by the river."

"Okay."

He cocked his head. "No, really. I want you to see me as a human being."

"I do, I swear."

His mouth dropped open, and it was her voice that came out: "He's deader than a doornail, Lieu." He grinned.

"Sir—"

"Stop calling me sir. My name's Travis."

"Okay, Travis. I'm sorry you died."

"Yeah, yeah. You're sorry about a lot of things."

"It's just that … I mean … I see a lot of dead people. If I allowed myself to be sad every time, I wouldn't be able to get through a day. It's not that I don't care, I just have to separate my work from my emotions."

"Hmph. Well, I don't completely understand, but I get what you're saying, I guess."

Feeling like she should try to show some empathy, she asked, "What were you like before you fell in the water?"

He chuckled and shook his head. "I appreciate the effort, doll. But lip service ain't gonna cut it. I know you don't *really* care."

"No. But I do."

He rolled his eyes. "All right, sure. Whatever. That's not why I'm here, anyways."

"No?"

He scoffed and looked out the driver's window. Then he turned back. "I need a favor."

"There's nothing I can do. You've been dead for too long."

"Not that."

"Then what?"

"You see, I'm married. I mean … was married … Or still. I don't know how this works." He wrinkled his forehead. "Our vows said until death do us part, so I guess maybe I'm not married anymore." He cocked his head in thought. Then he looked at her again and asked, "What do you think? Am I still married?"

Toni timidly nodded. She whispered, "I think so. And I bet your wife is frantic right now." As she said it, she wondered if that's what he wanted from her— to go to his house and comfort his grieving widow. Maybe tell her something for him.

He rubbed his head. "Anyway, doll, I'm worried about her and I need you to do me a solid."

"I don't know if I'm the right person for this."

"Just listen for a minute. I need you to go to my house in the morning when you get off work and—"

"I'm not a grief counselor. Isn't there someone else who would be mor—"

His eyes narrowed and an angry scowl twisted his features. "Listen to me," he snapped, sending a cold jolt through her bones. His dead eyes locked onto hers again and she couldn't turn away. "Tomorrow morning you are going to my house. Do you understand?"

She nodded, unable to stop herself.

"You will know what to do once you get there. Do you understand?"

Toni continued nodding helplessly.

The brief storm of anger passed and his smile returned. "I appreciate you doing this for me. I live at 1627 Forester Street. Do you know where that is?"

She shook her head.

"Do you have GPS on your phone?"

She nodded.

"Perfect. Now, put the address in your phone and I'll see you tomorrow." He snapped his fingers and it echoed like thunder.

Toni flinched and opened her eyes to someone beating on the passenger window.

"Toni," Steve shouted from outside.

Her eyes shot to the empty driver's seat. She reached for her door handle and gave it a tug. The locks clunked and the door popped open.

"What are you doing in there?" Steve asked. "I've been pounding on the window for ages. I was about to break it."

"I'm sorry. I just … um … I was just getting the report book and I think I zoned out."

"That's a nice way to put it. I'd say you were possessed or something. You really didn't know I was out here?"

She shook her head.

He looked at her sideways before circling the medic truck and climbing into the driver's seat. He shifted the truck into gear. Before he let off the brake, he turned to her. "Are you okay? You look like you've seen a ghost."

"I'm okay. I just feel bad for Travis."

"Who?"

"Oh. Uh … He's just someone I know. He had a rough day a few weeks ago and I was just thinking about him."

Steve shook his head. "I don't know what's gotten into you today."

"I'm just hungry, I think. I left late this morning and missed breakfast."

As they drove back to the station, Toni didn't get one word written of her report as she repeated Travis's address over and over in her mind. Once back at the station she put the address into her phone so she wouldn't forget.

2

Toni couldn't stop thinking about Travis throughout the rest of her shift and into the next morning. She had no idea what she was going to say to his grieving wife and couldn't understand why he had chosen her to do it. No matter how hard she tried to focus, she couldn't get her mind on her work. Steve had probably asked a dozen times if she was all right.

After a long night of dread, the change of shift finally arrived. She switched out of her uniform and rushed to her car. Her hands trembled as she pulled up Travis's address in the GPS on her phone and drove to his house.

She pulled up next to an empty driveway at 1627 Forester Street and parked next to the mailbox. She sat in her car for fifteen minutes before she found the courage to get out. Her feet were anvils, weighing down each step. It took all her will and strength just to make it to the porch.

A row of knee-high candy cane decorations lined the sidewalk. She cringed, knowing she was about to ruin some poor woman's Christmas. Her hand hovered near the door knocker.

"Go on," a voice startled her from behind.

She spun to find Travis standing on the porch behind her. He was an even bigger man than he'd appeared to be when sitting in the medic. Her hand shot to her chest.

He looked around nervously. "Go on," he said. "Knock." He reached for her hand and gently guided it back to the door.

She knocked and then stepped back so she wouldn't be right in his wife's face when she answered. "What's her name?" she whispered.

"Jessica," he said.

No one came to the door, so Toni knocked again. Still nothing. She turned to Travis and shrugged. "I don't think she's home. Now what?"

"I hope something didn't happen to her. You know, she might be grief-stricken and all. You should go in and make sure she's all right." There was something strange about his tone.

"How? I can't break in. We should call 9-1-1."

"No," he snapped, making her jump again. He paused and took a calming breath. Then he smiled. "Check under the mat. We keep an extra key there."

"I don't know about this, Travis."

He locked his blank eyes on hers and held her gaze. "I'm giving you permission to go into my home. I want you to go in now." He looked around again, breaking his hypnotic stare.

Static filled her mind. It seemed wrong, but she couldn't help herself. "Are you sure?"

"I am."

She knelt and lifted the corner of the mat to reveal a key. Travis nudged her forward. She grabbed the key and stuck it into the lock. Then she gave the knob a turn.

The door nudged open. She glanced back.

Travis nodded. "Go on." She pushed the door open. Her stomach turned and her knees went weak. She lost her breath and stumbled backward a step, bumping into Travis. He shoved her into the house and pulled the door shut behind him.

The room was covered in blood. An end table was overturned, and the TV mounted to the wall had an empty flower vase lodged in the broken screen. There was blood on it too.

Toni's terrified eyes widened. "What happened in …?"

Travis locked the front door and walked deeper into the room. Once he reached the center, he bowed his head and closed his eyes. He shook his head and whispered, "Why, Jason? Why did you have to say those things?"

Toni grabbed the doorknob and fumbled with the lock, but it spun freely and didn't release. She rattled the handle to no avail. She turned back and pressed her spine against the door.

Travis casually strolled through the room, his hand dragging along the bloodstained wall until he came to a stop by a stack of new paint cans and painting supplies. "We were going to paint the room together." He spoke so low that she couldn't tell if he was speaking to her or himself.

"What's going on?" she cried.

Travis paused and then turned his head toward her. His dead eyes locked with hers again. "I told you I needed your help."

"But your wife. Where is she? Did you kill her?"

His eyes went crooked. "What? I would never hurt her. She's probably at home right now grieving."

"But I thought *this* was your home." Terror rose from her gut.

Travis chuckled. "I don't live here. This is my friend Jason's house."

"Who's Jason?"

"Never mind that." He turned away.

Toni tilted her head. He almost looked embarrassed or ashamed. When he picked up a picture frame from a stand in the corner and gently caressed the image of a man, she put the pieces together.

She whispered, "He's your lover, isn't he?"

Travis hesitated and then nodded once.

Toni took in the room. "Travis, what did you do?"

It seemed difficult for him to answer. Finally, he whispered, "I hit him with the vase." Then he pointed to the bloody carpet. "This is where he fell." He bowed his head and mumbled, "Why, Jason? Why'd you have to threaten to tell her? Why'd you have to make me so mad?" He looked back to Toni. "He knew about my temper."

"So, he was going to tell your wife about your affair?"

He nodded, and she saw tears in his eyes.

"And you killed him for it?"

He nodded again and buried his face in his hands. "I didn't mean to."

"Travis, what am I doing here?"

He glanced over his shoulder. "You're going to clean up this mess before the police come snooping around."

Toni shook her head. "Oh no. I'm not doing that. In a million years I wouldn't do that. I—"

Travis spun. His face darkened and he shot across the room without his feet ever touching the floor. He had her shoulders in his iron grip before she could flinch. His dead eyes held her helpless gaze. "YOU WILL HELP ME," he bellowed inches from her face.

Toni couldn't breathe; she had forgotten how. "Travis, let go. You're hurting me."

His grip loosened and he sighed.

"I don't understand. Why do you want me to clean

this up? There's nothing they can do to you now."

He shook his head and walked away. With his back to her, he asked, "Do you really think I want my wife and kids to know the things I've done? They can never know about Jason. They wouldn't understand."

"But you killed him."

"I didn't mean to. He always pressed my buttons when we fought." He plopped onto the couch as if exhausted. "I loved him."

"Then you should let me tell the authorities what happened."

He shook his head. "I can't. I love my family, too. This would devastate them. No one would ever know if I hadn't fallen in that damn river before I could come back and clean up this mess."

"What about *his* family? Won't they come looking for him? Don't you care about how worried they'll be?"

"They disowned him a long time ago. I was the only family he had. That's why he wanted us to start a life together. Trust me. There's nobody looking for him."

"What about work. Didn't he have a job? Won't they wonder where he's been?"

He continued shaking his head. "He was laid off. Electrician. I was helping him with his rent."

Toni walked past him. She wanted to tell him again that she would never help him clean up a crime scene, but she couldn't form the words. Even as she silently argued with her conscience, she found herself digging through cleaning supplies in the hallway closet. It was as if she wasn't in control of her own actions. Travis watched from the couch as she washed the bloody surfaces with bleach. A single tear rested on his cheek. When she righted the end table beside the couch, he turned his head and stared at the wall beside the TV. He didn't move.

After hours of scrubbing the carpet and painting the walls to cover the stains, it was clean enough that nothing short of a forensic evaluation would find any evidence of a crime.

"I think I'm done," she finally said.

He smiled and stood up, putting a hand on the TV. "I bought this for him, you know." His smile faded. "We need to take it down."

"I don't know how."

"I do. There's a small toolbox under the kitchen sink. Go get it."

Once the TV was free of the wall mount, she placed it by the door along with the cleaning and paint supplies.

"Are we finished?" she asked.

He shook his head. "Go to the bedroom and pack a suitcase. It's in the closet."

She scowled. "Why pack a suitcase?"

"Jason was a grifter before he settled here. When his landlord comes to see why he hasn't paid the rent, it needs to look like he skipped town. No one will ever be the wiser."

She followed Travis to the bedroom, protesting the whole way. With his dead eyes watching her every move, she got the giant suitcase from the closet and packed it full of whatever Travis told her to. He left the room as soon as she was finished. When she turned to follow him, a swing set in the neighbor's yard caught her eye through the window. A sick feeling twisted her insides and she looked away. Swing sets gave her the creeps, though she could never remember why.

She hurried back to the front room where Travis

was waiting. He grinned.

Knowing that what she was doing was wrong, she searched deep for the strength to defy him. "I'm not going anywhere with you," she declared. "I can't be a part of this anymore. I don't even know how you got me to do this much."

Travis's face darkened and he grabbed the back of her neck with lightning speed. She tried to get away, but the pain chased her. He forced her head up so she could see his eyes. The flames of hell danced within them.

"You really shouldn't make me so angry. You aren't finished helping me quite yet. Is that understood?"

Her eyes drifted toward the freshly painted wall and her mind turned fuzzy. She couldn't think straight. He snarled slightly. She looked back at him and nodded.

He released her neck and the flames burned out in his lifeless eyes. "Gooood. Now, load everything in your car."

She put the cleaning supplies in the trunk first. Then the broken TV and the paint cans and brushes. The suitcase had to go on the back seat. Almost in a trance, she locked the front door, replaced the key under the mat, and climbed into her car.

Though it felt like her hands grabbing the steering wheel and her foot pressing the gas pedal, a look down revealed Travis's tennis shoe and thick, muscular hands. Her left ring finger had a wedding band.

She drove for an hour to an area she had never seen before and turned onto an equally unfamiliar dirt road. Dirt roads gave her the creeps, too. She was miles away from any houses or signs of civilization.

Then she spotted a minivan in the middle of nowhere. She didn't know why she pulled up next to it and stopped, but somehow knew she was in the right place. She looked in her rearview mirror and saw Travis standing behind her car looking across a field to the forest beyond. She had a fleeting urge to slam her car into reverse and plow him over, but her body wouldn't obey. Not that it would have done any good. Instead, she opened her door and climbed out.

Travis gazed longingly at the clouds. "It's such a beautiful day," he said.

She shivered and rubbed her arms.

He glanced over. "Oh, I guess it would be pretty cold for you, huh?"

"Freezing. It's not for you?"

"It is. But it has been since I fell in the river. Nothing can warm me now." He started toward the forest. "Come on."

"Is that Jason's van?"

He shook his head. "Nah. I dumped Jason's car in a pond before I came here. That's my van."

"What are you going to do with it?"

"When we're finished here, you're going to take it to Stevens Park near where you found my body. You know where that is?"

She nodded.

"Just leave it there. It'll look like I fell in the water while walking the trails."

"But you fell in weeks ago."

"It'll be months before someone realizes my van hasn't moved. Don't you worry about that." He started across the field.

She followed. As they walked, she asked, "Why are you doing this to me?"

"I'm not doing anything to you. You're helping

me. Remember? Just like the others you helped when you were a child."

A devastating image of a young boy hanging by a noose from a swing set flashed past her eyes. She staggered backward and nearly fell. "What did you say?"

He looked over his shoulder as he continued walking.

Toni swallowed hard and hurried to catch up. "I don't understand. Who else have I helped like this?"

He entered the tree line. "They told me about you."

"*Who*?"

He smirked. "You know who."

"I don't know what you're talking about. I've never had anything like this happen to me before."

"Yeah, right. Not even during the blackouts?"

A sledgehammer hit her in the chest. Growing up, she'd suffered from frequent blackouts that lasted anywhere from hours to days. She had no memory of them other than waking up in strange places with no clue how she had gotten there. One time she had woken up next to a dumpster behind a gas station late at night in a part of town she'd never been to before. Her frantic mother said she had been missing for hours, but Toni couldn't remember anything after getting off the school bus that afternoon. Two years later, just after her sweet sixteen, she'd woken up beside a dirt road in the middle of nowhere, holding a roll of duct tape and a flashlight. She'd lost a whole day that time.

"H-h-how did you know about my blackouts? I was just a kid. The doctors said they were psychosomatic."

"And you believed them?" He chuckled. "Whatever helps you sleep at night, doll." He stopped and scanned the area. "We're here."

They were near a riverbank. The body of man partially covered in snow lay next to a hole and a shovel. He was thin and young, and part of his left arm appeared to have been gnawed away.

"Is that Jason?"

Travis frowned and cocked his head. "How many people do you think I killed?" He knelt next to Jason's body and took his hand. He whispered something that Toni couldn't hear.

"Are you going to kill me?" she asked.

He shook his head without looking back at her.

Beside the shovel were a dark shirt and a pair of gray sweatpants in a pile. Travis caught Toni looking at them. "His blood was on 'em. I was getting ready to burn them when I took a step back and slipped down the bank." He pointed to the steep drop-off. "That's where I fell in the stupid river." He shook his head. "I knew I should have learned to swim when I was a kid."

He stood up and approached Toni. Their eyes locked. "Leave your keys here on the ground and go get the other stuff."

She turned to do as ordered, but he stopped her. "You should know Jason wasn't a helpless victim." He curled his upper lip, revealing his missing tooth. "He got a couple good shots on me, too."

"And that makes this okay?"

He shook his head. "Not really. I just wanted you to know I'm not a complete monster."

Toni didn't know what to say to that.

It took her three long trips, but eventually the TV, paint supplies, suitcase, and cleaning supplies were gathered near the hole. "I don't have any matches," she said.

Travis pointed to the pile of clothes. "I do. They're by my sweatpants. Like I said, I was about to burn them when I ... well, you know."

Toni burned all the evidence while Travis stood and watched with his dead, hypnotic eyes. She warmed her numb hands by the fire until it burned down to smoldering ashes. Then she shoved everything into the hole with Jason's body and shoveled the dirt overtop.

"Are you ready for the next step?" Travis asked.

"Where now? I thought I was done."

"We have to get rid of my van, remember?"

Toni was too tired to argue. When she got to his van and climbed in, he was already in the passenger seat.

"Stevens Park, right?" she asked in a defeated monotone.

He smiled.

Once they reached the park, he guided her to a parking spot at the farthest end of the lot. "Just leave it here with the keys under the seat."

"Is that it?"

He nodded.

"How am I going to get my car?"

"Call an Uber. I'll ride back with you." He reached over and touched her shoulder. "You did well, Toni. Thank you."

She nodded. She left his keys under his seat, climbed out, and closed the door. She walked a good distance from the park to a small neighborhood before calling for an Uber.

Her ride arrived within the hour. She didn't speak to the driver other than to tell him where to go. Travis sat quietly beside her the whole way. The driver didn't ask any questions and left her next to her car.

Once he was gone, Travis walked with her back to Jason's grave. They sat on a fallen tree for what felt like hours without speaking. Finally, Travis sighed. "I'm sorry I had to use you like that." He stood up.

She nodded. "Are you leaving now?"

"Yes."

"Before you leave, will you tell me what you meant about my blackouts?"

"You're what we call a helper, Toni. Do you remember knowing a kid named Jacob when you were little?"

"Vaguely. He went to my school. He died in an accident. He got his neck caught in a rope when he was playing on some playground equipment."

"He's one of the ones who told me about you. You don't remember helping him?"

She shook her head.

"Jacob killed himself. He didn't want his parents to know, and you helped him cover it up. You untied the noose and made it look like he got tangled up while pretending to be Spider-Man or something. You really don't remember?"

She shook her head. "Not really. Just flashes here and there."

"And you won't remember helping me, either." He stood up. "I'm sorry I have to do this. The others won't be happy about it." His ice-cold finger touched her chin and lifted her eyes to his one last time. "Toni, from now until you die you will believe that you are the one responsible for killing Jason and hiding his body. As far as you know, you met him at a bar and had one of your blackouts, and then you woke up here."

"Oh, no-no-no-no. You can't do this to me. You *can't*."

"Someone besides me has to take the blame if his body is ever found."

"But they'll never believe I did it … Will they?"

"You better hope not. It's your fingerprints at his house. It was your car in front of his home all day. It was your Uber ride out here. If you do go down for helping me, well, I'm sorry."

"Why are you doing this?"

"I already told you. My wife and kids can never know what I did."

"What if I tell them?"

"Tell them what? You aren't going to remember me as anything more than a body you pronounced dead when I was pulled from the river."

A tear slipped down her cheek.

Travis wiped it away with his knuckle. "Again, I'm sorry I had to do this to you, Toni."

She looked up with heartbroken eyes. "What do I do now?"

"That's up to you. You can choose to tell the authorities what you think you've done, but there's a good chance no one will ever find out unless you tell them. You can remain free for as long as you keep our secret."

She nodded, sniffling as the tears started flowing freely. When she looked up again, he was gone. Her eyes went to the fresh grave and she couldn't believe she had killed someone. Though everything was twisted and blurry in her mind, she vaguely remembered meeting Jason at a bar. She hadn't blacked out like this in years. Why now? She sat on the log until her toes were numb and her cheeks stung from the cold. It was getting dark.

Eventually, she found the strength to stand up. Her stomach twisted every time she thought about what she had done to poor Jason. She wouldn't even believe she could do such a thing if there wasn't still dirt under her fingernails. No matter how hard she tried, she couldn't remember anything after leaving the bar.

She walked to the edge of the bank overlooking the river. The water rushed by, promising an end to her guilt and suffering, and all she had to do was take one more step. Her toes hung over the edge. It's what she deserved for what she'd done.

Then the ground gave way beneath her left foot. Her ass hit the bank and her hand caught a tree root by luck. Maybe bad luck. Her legs dangled just above the rushing water. She dragged herself away from the edge and back onto solid ground.

After lying in the cold snow and staring at the sky until the full moon had risen, she decided she didn't want to die. She pulled herself to her feet, knelt over Jason's grave, and whispered, "I'm so sorry."

During her drive home, she was never so scared to be pulled over in her life. She was exhausted when her head finally hit her pillow just before sunrise.

When she woke again, she opened her eyes with a start. A wave of guilt rushed through her and she remembered what she had done to poor Jason. She ran to the bathroom and threw up in the toilet. Then she sat hugging the rim for a lifetime. "I'm so sorry, Jason," she cried. She would never forgive herself.

3

It had been two years since Toni had killed and
buried a stranger named Jason, and not a day went by
that the guilt didn't chew on her insides. She had lost
enough weight for her coworkers to be concerned and
her indigestion was a nightmare some days, but she
told herself that it was her punishment for what she
had done.

In her mind, every police cruiser she saw could be
the one finally looking for her. But as much as she
wanted to tell them about what she had done and end
her sleepless nights, she feared prison even more than
the guilt.

Today was her first day at a new station after
transferring for the seventh time since she'd worked
on Medic 14 with Steve. She couldn't seem to fit in
anywhere anymore. Steve was sad when she left, but
she couldn't look him in the eye knowing what she
had done.

She sat in her car in the parking lot, trying to build
the courage to go inside and meet her new crew. She
was hopeful this new station would work out. She had
heard good things about the new lieutenant there.
Having a good lieutenant was crucial.

It was ten minutes before roll call when she found
the strength to go inside. She took a deep breath, got
her firefighter gear from her trunk, and headed in.
The lieutenant was already in the bay getting his own

gear in order beside the fire engine. She went over to introduce herself. His helmet was bright red, proving he was indeed a new lieutenant and hadn't yet had many fires since getting promoted. Some of the more grizzled veteran lieutenants' helmets were charred and black.

He looked up as she approached.

She set her bag down and extended her hand. "Hi. I'm Toni. I guess I'll be working for you now."

He shook her hand. "Hi, Toni. It's nice to meet you. I'm—"

"I know who you are, Lieu," she interrupted. "I saw you at the hospital after you saved those two kids. You just got promoted out of Twenty-two's recently, didn't you?"

"Yep. That's me. I guess I'll be stationed here for a while. I look forward to working with you."

"It's nice to meet you, Lieu."

He waved his hand. "Just call me Elliot. We're all friends here."

She started to ask him where he wanted her on the truck when the tones blared and the dispatcher reported an auto accident.

"Should we take that run for them?" she asked. She knew firefighters hated taking runs right before it was time to get off duty because it could tie them up for hours.

Elliot nodded.

The off-going crew filed into the bay. Toni and Elliot met them.

"We can take that run for you guys," Elliot said.

The lieutenant he was replacing answered, "Awesome. I've got a doctor's appointment this morning and I've had to reschedule twice already."

The third member of Elliot's crew was already

jumping into the driver's seat. Toni threw her bag in the back seat while Elliot climbed up front. With the off-going crew clear of the truck and the bay door opened, the driver floored it.

The driver glanced back. "I'm Scott," he shouted. He had a bushy handlebar mustache and a buzzed head.

She nodded and politely waved. "Toni."

"Nice to meet you, Toni."

She put her fire gear on while they weaved through morning traffic. By the time they reached the scene, she was dressed and ready to work.

A semi-truck with a smashed front end sat facing a twisted metal monstrosity that might have once been a car. Bystanders regarded the accident with horrified stares.

"I think she's dead," someone shouted as Elliot hopped out.

Toni was reaching for the door when a sinking feeling grabbed hold of her gut. She hesitated. There was someone else in the truck.

A woman's voice said, "Hey."

Toni spun toward the other seat where a young woman now sat. She appeared sad and distraught, and her blond hair was matted down with blood.

"Who are you?" Toni cried.

"I think I just died over there. They said you could help me. I made a terrible mistake."

Toni sank into the seat. Panic coursed through her veins. She looked outside and the world was frozen. "No, no, no," she moaned. "What's happening?"

The memory of sitting on a felled tree near Jason's grave flooded her brain. But something was different about it than the thousand other times she'd remembered being there. This time she wasn't alone.

There was a man in sweats with a missing front tooth sitting beside her. A name flashed in her mind.

Travis.

The young woman waved her hand in front of Toni's face and snapped her fingers. "Yoo-hoo," she said.

"What do you want?"

The young woman tilted her head. "I did something very bad. I need your help."

"No," Toni cried through trembling lips. "I can't. I won't."

The young woman grinned and locked eyes with her. "Nonsense. It will only take a few minutes. You won't remember a thing."

Toni covered her face and screamed.

END

Subscribe to Epertase for news, updates, and future announcements.

ABOUT THE AUTHOR

Douglas R. Brown is a fantasy and horror writer living in Pataskala, Ohio. He began writing as a cathartic way of dealing with the day-to-day stresses of life as a firefighter/paramedic in Columbus, Ohio. Now he focuses his writing on fantasy and horror, where he can draw from his lifelong love of the genres. He has been married since 1996 and has a son. He has had four books published to date, including his werewolf tale with a twist, *Tamed*, and his fantasy trilogy, *The Light of Epertase*. Though the publishing company ultimately closed its doors, Douglas has given his work a new home under his own imprint of Epertase Publishing. This is his second self-published title under Epertase Publishing following the fantasy novel *Death of the Grinderfish*. Visit Douglas at www.epertasepublishing.com or email him your thoughts at epertase@gmail.com.

Also by the Author

Death of the Grinderfish

Tamed

The Light of Epertase Trilogy Including Legends Reborn

A Kingdom's Fall

The Rise of Cridon

Printed in Great Britain
by Amazon

72648339R00156